BLOODLINES

WRAK-ASHWEA: THE AGE OF LIGHT
BOOK TWO

LEIGH ROBERTS

DRAGON WINGS PRESS

Editing by Joy Sephton: http://www.justemagine.biz
Cover design by Cherie Fox: http://www.cheriefox.com

Sexual activities in this book are intended for adults.

ISBN: 978-1-951528-40-9 (ebook)
ISBN: 978-1-951528-41-6 (paperback)

CONTENTS

Dedication

For those whose hearts are brave enough to step into the possibility of...

What If?

CHAPTER 1

An'Kru was only days away from turning seven, and no one was more aware of this than Adia. His surreal visit to her years ago had immensely helped her deal with his leaving to go with Pan and the unique nature of his life path. She had only ever shared it with Acaraho, and it had helped him immensely as well.

Even from the moment he was born, An'Kru had never been an ordinary offspring. He didn't have the unfocused gaze of a newling but of someone with life experience. He began speaking later than others his age, but when he did start talking, he spoke like an adult. There was no offspring-talk; it was as if he simply stepped into a later stage of development. From the time he began to speak, he didn't call Adia Mama or Amara, but Mother. All of Etera's creatures were still drawn to him, but he had somehow learned to control their awareness of his presence, and they did not automatically flock to him every time he was outside.

Adia had early on given up getting him to eat any type of meat or fish. He simply refused it no matter how it was offered.

"He never complains," Adia said one day to her friend Eyota as they were sitting watching their offspring play together in the shallows.

"I noticed that. He seems to have a grateful heart."

They watched as Aponi, Nelairi, Tansy, and An'Kru took turns tossing stones across the water, seeing who could make one skip the most times. Each time one of them giggled or laughed, both mothers smiled.

"I hate to bring it up, but you are heavy on my mind nowadays," Eyota said.

"You are referring to An'Kru and Nootau leaving soon?"

"Yes."

"I am at peace with it, though when the actual time comes, I am sure it will be very hard to see them leave. But they are very close to each other, and in an odd way, it helps that An'Kru seems so mature," Adia shared. "He does not seem as vulnerable as others his age, if that makes sense. And Nootau will be there with him. Wherever *there* is.

"I do feel for Iella, though," she added. "In all this

time, she and Nootau still have not had offspring. Even though the People are not very prolific, I think many of us now believe Nootau's fertility was impacted by the contagion that swept through here so long ago."

"Iella is so good with the offspring; it would be a shame if they never have any," Eyota frowned. "And without Nootau here—"

"Their settling at the High Rocks was such a blessing," Adia said. "Iella has turned out to be a very fine Healer, though there was no doubt she would be. And Apricoria as well, under Urilla Wuti's tutorship." She sighed. "It has been relatively peaceful these last six years, other than the escalation of the Waschini against the Brothers. I prayed for a sense of routine to return, and it has. And I have done my best to cherish every moment."

Just then, all the offspring came running quickly, An'Kru in front. He was holding something in his hands. Adia and Eyota peered over as he slowly opened them to reveal a snow-white butterfly. The insect opened and closed its wings in a beautiful display. Even its eyes were white. Such delicate creatures were seen occasionally, but something about this one sent a shiver up Adia's spine.

"A symbol of transformation, of grace," Eyota said, glancing at Adia. "And the ability to accept change."

The Healer said a silent prayer of thanks to the

Great Mother for this reminder and reassurance delivered to her so clearly.

Adia had done her best to prepare Aponi and Nelairi for when their older brother would leave the High Rocks. She had explained to them that he had a different path awaiting him and that his soul would not be at rest if he didn't walk it. The three of them were very close to each other and Nootau. She knew that when Nootau and An'Kru left, it would affect the twins deeply. No matter how she tried to prepare them, they would grieve such a significant absence.

CHAPTER 2

The passing years had brought many changes. But what had not changed was the good will between the Akassa, Sassen, the Brothers, and the few Waschini who had been brought into their circle. The brotherhood that had formed between them all was stronger than ever, helped by Ned and Awantia's mission to teach Whitespeak to as many of the Brothers as they could reach.

"We have visited all the Brothers' villages that anyone knows about," Ned explained to Acaraho.

"To venture out into unknown territory would be dangerous. Not everyone welcomes a Waschini—or one of the Brothers," said the Leader. "And it is even more dangerous considering that we continue to hear of the escalation of the Waschini acts against the Brothers. Fortunately, they have left alone those living on Oh'Dar's Morgan Trust property. But we do not know how long that protection will hold up. It is now for the Brothers to select people from among their own to continue reaching out to the other Chiefs when they have their pau-waus to visit, celebrate, and share stories. Just as they have spread the word about the coming Age of Light."

"So, then, our work teaching Whitespeak is done. After a short stay, we will return home to Chief Kotori's village. But Awantia and I want to visit with Oh'Dar and his family before we leave. I regret I have never been able to take her home to meet my family," Ned said. "But I feared it might put her in danger. I do need to return soon as it has been so long, and I promised to try to return at least once a year. It is hard to be away from my parents as they are getting older, and I barely know my nieces and nephews.

When Ned and Awantia began to travel to the other villages, they were together constantly, depending on each other for survival. Their companionship deepened their respect for each other, and they shared many light-hearted times together. One evening as they were sitting next to each other by the fire, Ned had once again brought up Awantia's lack of a mate.

"So, have you met anyone in our travels who might be a potential life-walker?"

"This again?" she laughed. "I swear if it is not Myrica trying to match me with someone, then it is you. No, no one has caught my eye. I am happy doing what we do."

"Just as well for you. It is painful to care for someone when they do not return your feelings."

"I am sorry, Ned Webb. Many are enamored with Myrica, but she does not return their interest either. Please do not take it personally."

"I am not speaking of Myrica."

Awantia had looked down, saddened to hear that someone other than Myrica had touched his heart. She didn't want to know, but she also did. So she plucked up her courage and asked, "So, who is this woman who has won her way into your heart?"

She felt a hand touch her chin, startling her. She looked over at him, and he soothed her cheek with the back of his hand. She was caught off guard but did not pull away. Then Ned said, "How is it, with all the time we have spent together, that you do not know?"

Awantia froze, and Ned leaned in and kissed her. She drew back, a frown crossing her face.

"I am sorry," Ned quickly apologized. "I had no right. But I had to take a chance. I can not live my life any longer not knowing, unable to quench the fire burning in my heart, hoping that you might secretly care for me after all—as I care for you." Ned rose to his feet to walk away.

Awantia stood up as quickly as she could. "No, please," she pleaded. "Let me speak."

Ned stopped walking but didn't turn back. "It is late," he said, "we should both turn in."

"It is time I tell you the truth," Awantia said. "You have a right to know."

"It is none of my business," Ned said, but he reluctantly turned to face her.

"But it is. A while ago, we had a similar conversation, and I told you it was improper to ask, so you have said nothing of it again. Therefore, the fault is mine. I should never have let things go this long without talking about it."

"It is fine, really. People cannot help who they love—or do not love."

"No, you misunderstand me," she said.

Ned frowned, "What? What are you saying?"

"I am saying that all this time, I believed it was Myrica you cared for. It did not occur to me that you might have feelings for me. But I have cared for you for a long time. I love you, Ned Webb. And if you really want me, then of all men, you would be welcome at my fire. Every night, for as long as we both walk this life."

Ned quickly closed the space between them and swept her into his arms. "My prayers have been answered."

"So have mine," Awantia exclaimed. She looked into his eyes as he kissed her again, this time long and slow. She felt his heartbeat against hers. She wanted him never to let her go.

When they returned to their home village, they went first to Awantia's father and mother to tell them. Her mother was happy, knowing that her daughter would have a man at her fire and, hopefully soon, children. Ned had earned her father's respect, so he approved of the joining. After that, word traveled quickly that Ned and Awantia were to be bonded. It surprised some but not others. Many of the elderly women simply smiled and looked at each other, nodding as if a secret they had shared together was now openly exposed. But the one most shocked of all was Myrica. A few days later, at one of their evening fires, when it was just the two young women, Myrica plied Awantia for more detail.

"All this time, you were trying to interest me in the Waschini. Why would you do that if you cared for him yourself?"

"I never believed he would grow to care for me. And I truly believed he would make a fine provider and life-walker. I wanted you to find happiness."

Myrica was touched by what she realized must have been a deep sacrifice on Awantia's part. To give up the man she loved, so her friend could be happy?

"Oh, my dear friend," Myrica leaned over and hugged Awantia. "How can anyone's heart be so pure and unselfish? I am so very happy for you both."

Oh'Dar's family had also grown. In addition to I'Layah, he and Acise now had two sons, born fairly close together. Where I'Layah favored Oh'Dar's side, their sons favored their mother. Both had the Brothers' straight black hair and brown eyes, though their skin was a tone between their parents. There having been no more trouble at the village, the family had gone back to spending a lot of their time there, though Oh'Dar made sure they all spent plenty of time with Miss Vivian and Ben, who were advancing in years. Both had lived far longer than most Waschini, for which Oh'Dar was deeply grateful, but the reality of their ages was never far from his mind.

"In a few years," Miss Vivian said, "I'Layah will be able to go with you to the Webbs."

Oh'Dar picked out his grandmother's favorite foods from his breakfast and gave them to her. "Yes. Acise and I agree with you and Ben. I know you have educated her as much as you can about the white world, but she needs to experience it first-hand. Unlike Tsonakwa and Ashova, in time, she will be able to blend in without suspicion."

"She is smart, just like her brothers," Ben said. "She has absorbed all your grandmother has taught her so far. Her English is impeccable, as is her writing. And her reading level is progressing strongly as well. No one will question her schooling."

"It is still a few years off, but when the time is right, it will happen," Oh'Dar agreed.

His grandmother suggested, "Maybe she can stay with the Webbs for a summer. I am sure they would take good care of her, especially Grace, since she and Newell have their own children now."

She sighed, "In time, someone will need to take over my documentation of the People's history."

"You know I don't like it when you talk like that."

"You must face it, son," Ben added. "We are both pretty old."

Oh'Dar looked away briefly. "It will probably be me. Perhaps when I'Layah is old enough and mature enough to handle the content, she can take it over."

"I also started a journal long ago. Did I tell you that?" Miss Vivian asked.

"Yes. I assume it is stored with the historical records?"

"It is. In time, perhaps I'Layah will keep one of her own."

Miss Vivian shivered suddenly. "Lately, it seems to be growing colder here all the time." Oh'Dar got up and rearranged the colorful knitted shawl she had made and now carried everywhere with her. He pulled it up over her shoulders and gave her a kiss on the cheek. Both she and Ben seemed to be more and more affected by the cooler temperatures of

Kthama. And due to fatigue, they had begun spending less and less time in the general areas, mostly staying in their room or venturing out a short distance on very warm days. They seldom attended the High Council meetings, and others had taken over teaching Whitespeak to the offspring.

Oh'Dar tried to keep his mind off their decline.

"How are your parents doing?" Miss Vivian asked. Everyone was very aware that the time was approaching when the Guardian Pan would return to take An'Kru and Nootau with her.

"Both of them are doing remarkably well. Not saying they won't be sad, but I had expected my mother, at least, to be in a bad state by this time; Pan could return at any moment."

"It is almost time for me to return to Kthama for An'Kru and his brother Nootau," Pan told her mate, Rohm'Mok.

"I wonder how our people will react to having an Akassa among them again," he said. "I suspect it will bring back many bittersweet memories for those of us who lived among them and were called their Protectors."

"And how their presence will affect Moart'Tor. It will be a chance for him to get to know an Akassa first hand. But I think the focus will be on An'Kru's role, as so many hopes for Etera rest with him."

"How long will you be gone?"

"Not long. His mother knows this day is coming and has had years to prepare for it—as much as that is possible. Losing two of her sons, even for any amount of time, will be life-changing."

"Will you go alone?"

"Probably. In the past, I offered for Moart'Tor to go with me. But now the timing is wrong."

"I wondered if Moart'Tor would want to go."

"He did at the time we talked about it." Pan tilted her head. "What made you think to ask that?"

"You used to mention there was a sadness in him. Though it does seem he and his mate have grown closer in the past year or so."

Pan let out a sigh. "Yes, it is true. In my heart, I suspect he paired too soon. I believe he did so to move his life here forward. But at last, they do seem to be happy together."

Naha was due to deliver any time. She moved about their quarters, one hand on her belly, occupied with preparing the newling's nest. She had made some simple toys for the offling. One was a brownish toy in the approximate shape of a squirrel made from two pieces of hide glued together with tree resin.

It helped Moart'Tor to see his mate so light-hearted. He knew Naha longed for offling, as did most of the Mothoc females. He knew that this had been her primary motivation for pairing. In the years since they paired, one offling had been deadborn, which was heartbreaking. Knowing how much she had grieved losing it, Moart'Tor was relieved she was almost due to deliver. At last, she would have one of her own to cuddle, love, and protect.

"You really do not care if it is male or female?" Iria asked again as she fussed with the nest.

"I do not have a preference. It makes me happy to see you happy. Although you are going to wear out that nest before he or she even gets to use it," Moart'Tor teased his mate.

She smiled, "But you do not care? Truly?"

"I will welcome a son or a daughter. Both bring blessings of their own. Besides, offling sounds are joyful to me, even if they are crying."

"I am glad to hear that," Naha laughed. "No doubt, I will often remind you that you said it."

"Fair enough." In what had become a more frequent show of affection, he wrapped his arms around her from behind, gently rubbing her swollen belly.

"I hope he or she has your coloring," Nala continued.

"If it is a daughter, I am not sure I agree. It will

bring her too much attention from the males," he said.

"Our offling is not even born, and you are worrying about that?" she gently chided him. She turned and reached up to wrap her arms around his neck. All they had been through together had created a close bond, and they had grown to love each other.

"Tell me truthfully," she said. "Do you still think about Eitel?" Moart'Tor had told her about his stay with the Sassen at Kayerm and about Eitel, who tried to befriend him. Now he realized that Naha must have picked up on his feelings for her.

"I sometimes wonder what happened to her and hope she is happy. But not in a way that takes anything away from our pairing, if that is what you are asking."

"It was. Thank you. I cannot help it; when you spoke of her, I felt you had feelings for her—affection perhaps."

"I did. Some of it was affection, and some of it was regret over how I rebuffed her attempts to befriend me."

"The Guardian will be returning to Kthama soon to bring back the Promised One. Perhaps you could ask her to find out about Eitel, if it would bring you any relief?"

"I will ask because I feel, in a way, I wronged her,

but not because I want to be with her instead of you. Simply because I do still carry those regrets."

"I know. Oh, there were times in the beginning when I worried about it. But I believe what you are saying. Hopefully, she has paired by now and has a family of her own."

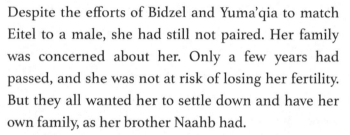

Despite the efforts of Bidzel and Yuma'qia to match Eitel to a male, she had still not paired. Her family was concerned about her. Only a few years had passed, and she was not at risk of losing her fertility. But they all wanted her to settle down and have her own family, as her brother Naahb had.

Naahb had asked for a match about a year after Moart'Tor left. Now he and his mate had a son whom they adored. In a few years, Naahb would start teaching his son about the patterns of the sky, the phases of the moon, and all the other things fathers had taught their sons since the time the Sassen were created by the Great Spirit out of the dust of Etera.

Eitel was out for a walk with Haaka, with whom she had become friends. Kalli was walking beside them, occasionally holding her mother's hand. Haaka carried her second daughter, Del'Cein, who was the result of Haaka's seeding by an Akassa male. Eitel had become part of the family, and the offling coaxed her to watch them when their mother had other things to attend to.

Nearing a pretty little clearing, Haaka set Del'-Cein down to let her walk around for a while. It slowed them down considerably as the young offling wanted to stop and examine everything. Kalli set out to play with her little sister while Haaka and Eitel sat to watch.

Del'Cein was too young to understand that Haan was not her blood father. In time Haaka would explain it to her. Kalli knew Haaka was not her birth mother, but it didn't seem to matter to her. At this age, it was just a detail and a curiosity more than anything else.

While Eitel was watching Del'Cein and Kalli play, Haaka's thoughts drifted back to how she finally became seeded by an Akassa.

Acaraho had made the plea for a male Akassa to seed Haaka at her request. He had explained that no physical contact would take place, and even though there would be no paternal participation in raising it, the offspring would, in time, be allowed to know who its father was. Adia later told Haaka she had been pleasantly surprised when her mate mentioned how many males had volunteered. After considering the volunteers, Adia and Acaraho agreed among themselves that Lannak'Sor would be the first candidate. But if the match was not agreeable to either party, the next in line would be introduced to Haaka, and so on.

Lannak'Sor was a robust, healthy male. He was one of the watchers and, when he was not on duty on the outskirts of the territory, lived among the bachelors of the High Rocks. Although in time, he hoped to pair, he had explained to Adia and Acaraho his reason for volunteering.

The day had come to meet the potential father, and Haaka paced nervously. Adia had assured her that if, after meeting him, she did not want to go through with it, there would be no ill feelings and that he also had the same option to change his mind.

"I know how important this is," Haaka had said to Adia. "It is a big commitment for all of us. Even though Haan and I will raise the offling, whoever this Akassa is will always know he is a father."

With everyone understanding their roles, Acaraho brought Lannak'Sor to meet Haaka.

She and the Akassa introduced themselves.

"I am willing to answer whatever you want to ask me," he began. "But first, let me say this; I grew up with the Healer's son, Oh'Dar. I saw how, in many ways, it was difficult for him to be the only one of his kind here. Even though your daughter Kalli's differences are not as obvious from the rest of us as Oh'Dar's are, I would like to be part of giving Kalli someone more like her to go through life with. Growing up, I had the benefit of siblings, and we are still close. Our parents are gone now, so all my brothers and sisters and I have now is each other."

Adia later told Haaka that she knew he meant what he had said. Even though some of Lannak'Sor's siblings were paired and had offspring of their own, the Akassa recognized how important the relationship between brothers and sisters was. And even more so when they were left to carry on without their mother and father.

In spite of herself, Haaka felt her cheeks burning. Even without the process requiring physical intimacy, it was still a very personal situation. She had no illusions that the Akassa might find her attractive, just as, in return, she did not find him attractive. Still.

"I know several things about you," she said. "What is mostly on my mind is whether you are prepared for how this might affect your life? I mean, later."

"In case I pair at some point?" Lannak'Sor asked. "I hope to. And I cannot imagine spending my life with someone who could not understand the importance of this situation. Or are you talking about when the offspring wants to know who his or her father is?"

Haaka said, "Both, really. But considering your answer to the first part, which I appreciate, then it would be the second part. Even if he or she is not different enough to realize my mate is not her blood father, they still would have a right to know the truth."

"I will be here for all of you, and especially our offspring."

Lannak'Sor's use of the term "our offspring" had brought the reality of what they were doing firmly to bear. Haaka had spoken with Haan at length about this, and she believed him when he said none of it would bother him and that he supported her decision. But what would the reality be? Would he truly feel this way later when it was not just a thought but became reality?

With Haaka and Lannak'Sor having agreed, preparations were made, and Haaka was in the Healer's Quarters waiting for her part of the process. Adia was with her, more for company than anything else, as Haaka knew what to do.

"What if it does not, take—for lack of a better word?" Haaka asked.

"Remember, we repeat this in a few days. Maybe three times in total. Then we have to wait to see if you are seeded. If not, we will try again. We must all be patient. Does Haan know today is the day?"

"He asked not to know the specific day and time. I do not think it is because it bothers him; I think he is just being considerate of my privacy. He asked me to tell him when I am seeded so he can return to my bed, that is all."

Within a little while, Nadiwani brought in a

shallow dish with a piece of wet moss in it. Adia and Nadiwani left, and Haaka lay on the sleeping mat, said a prayer, and inserted the piece of moss. She lay there for a while before removing and discarding it. Then she called for Adia and Nadiwani to come in.

"I have to believe you are right," Haaka said. "This is how the Ancients must have done it. There is no other way to become seeded by one of the brothers. Or an Akassa. But how they accomplished the first part, getting the male's seed, I have no idea."

"That knowledge is lost to us forever, I am afraid, but I am happy for you," said Adia.

Nadiwani agreed. "You can go about your day whenever you are ready. We will meet again in three days."

Later that week, they repeated the process. And then they waited. Finally, after several rounds of trying, Haaka was seeded.

When she had told Haan, Haaka said, "You have been so kind and supportive. I cannot thank you enough. Our family is growing. Kalli will soon have a brother or sister, and we have plenty of time to have more of our own."

"It is a good decision. I raised Akar'Tor though he was not of my blood. And I loved him as my own. You know I will do the same for this one. We will be one family."

Kalli and Del'Cein looked pretty much alike, and Haaka and Haan were thankful for that. Both tended toward the Akassa side but with a broader nose and thicker hair. As Kalli grew, she started looking more Akassa than Sassen, and Haaka wondered if that would happen with Del'Cein. Kalli's birth mother was Hakani, an Akassa. But Del'Cein's mother was Sassen, and her father was an Akassa. Haaka wondered how that might affect her new daughter's adult appearance. She didn't care which they favored; she just wanted them to look enough alike that neither felt she didn't fit in anywhere, as Akar'Tor had felt while living at Kayerm as the only Akassa.

Del'Cein's birth had opened again the question in many of the Sassen's minds, posed several years ago by Dorn.

"I mean no disrespect to Kalli," said Dorn as he nodded to the offling playing on the floor. "But is this our future?"

Kalli looked up when she heard her name.

Haan sighed. Haaka frowned at Dorn, who caught her expression.

"I— I apologize, Haaka," he stammered. "I— I realize that remark sounded critical."

Haaka reached down and picked up Kalli. "Is this so bad if it is our future? Yes, she looks more like the Akassa than the Sassen. But what does that matter? She is a sweet soul; she is an offling and deserves our love and protection no matter what she looks like. If we have to breed with the Akassa to survive, at least we will survive."

Dorn briefly looked up to the ceiling as if praying for a way to correct his blunder.

"Again, I apologize. But we need to discuss our future now that we are settling into a routine. We carry what is left of the Mothoc blood. If it is diluted even further, where does that leave Etera? Was that not the purpose of the Rah'hora? To keep our bloodline separate from that of the Akassa?"

"I do not know the answer, Dorn," said Haan. "It is true that crossing with the Akassa would further dilute the Mothoc blood. But if it is that or to disappear entirely, what choice do we have? Perhaps if we can increase our population, the numbers will compensate for the loss in concentration. I can only trust that hidden from our awareness, the Order of Functions is working this out as always."

Haaka thought of Hakani and Akar'Tor, two tortured souls who couldn't find their way. Both dead and buried, long returned to dust. She pictured them reunited in the Corridor Adia had talked about. She prayed they had both found peace at last.

She was brought out of her reminiscing and back to the present when Eitel spoke.

"Can you keep a secret?"

"Oh, yes! What?!"

"Well, you sound pretty excited; I am not sure you can keep it to yourself!" Eitel laughed.

"No, I promise. Please tell me."

"I think I am ready to be paired."

"Really? Oh, my! Have you told your parents? Your brother?"

"No, that is why it is a secret," she laughed.

"When did this change?"

Eitel sighed. "With the time I have spent with you and your offling and my brother and his family, I see how rich your lives are. I want that for myself. It is time to let the past go; my memories and daydreams of Moart'Tor are not enough. I should not have held onto them for so long."

"He has been gone a long time. There is no reason to believe he would be coming back. At least not here to live, I am sure."

"I know. And my brother was right; it would not have been a safe union. I could have died giving birth to any of our offling."

"Bidzel and Yuma'qia have found several matches for you. Are you finally going to ask who they are?"

"Yes. And I can then watch them from afar and see if I want to approach one."

"Surely, after all this time living at Kht'shWea, you will recognize them by their names?"

"I imagine. Oops!" Eitel pointed over to Haaka's daughters, who were wading in a little puddle, Kallie holding Del'Cein's hand. Del'Cein laughed and stomped her feet, splashing both herself and her sister.

"Oh, my! I thought the Akassa, too, did not like water!"

"You think of them as both Akassa?" Eitel asked.

"Yes, I do. They look far more Akassa than Sassen. They will most likely find mates among the People—if they do at all."

"Is that why you gave her an Akassa name?" Eitel asked.

"Yes. Just as Kalli is more of an Akassa name than a Sassen one."

Haaka got up to fetch her daughters before they fell down and made more of a mess. "I think we should go back. You need to talk to your parents and your brother."

"I will, but is there a reason I should rush?"

"Yes. This is too good a secret for me to keep to myself very long!" Haaka laughed.

"To finally let go of Moart'Tor, there is something I still need to do. So, to help you keep quiet, you have to tell me a secret now to make it even!" Eitel teased.

"Oh, alright. I guess that is a good idea. So—" Haaka paused.

"What? What?"

"Come closer," she said. Eitel leaned in, and Haaka whispered, "I am finally going to have Haan's offling!"

Haan was late getting back to their quarters and sat down as soon as he could. He had spent the day checking Kht'shWea with High Protector Qirrik and several helpers, clearing the paths from some rock falls. He was tired and, therefore, happy to see Haaka already had the offling fed and settled down.

He felt her come up behind him.

She wrapped her arms around his neck and kissed the side of his face. "You look tired."

"I am. But I appreciate having a family to come home to."

"I have some good news to share," she whispered into his ear.

He turned his head and smiled. "Oh? I could use some good news. What is it?"

"I am seeded. I am carrying your offling!"

Haan whipped around in his seat and exclaimed, "Really? Are you sure?"

"Yes, I am far enough along to know for sure, or I would not have told you."

He stood up and wrapped his arms around her. "We both thought it might never happen." Then he loosened his embrace and looked around, smiling. "We are going to need larger quarters. I will start looking around tomorrow."

Samuel Riggs did as Louis Morgan had told him. He stayed out of fights, kept his head down, and didn't talk back to the guards. He had washed more grimy prison dishes and handled more raw food than he could have imagined possible. He was also given one of the most prize roles, preparing food, thanks to Louis' favor—something that didn't go unnoticed by the other inmates. He could feel their resentment, so he stayed away from them as much as possible. Louis' protection only went so far. And there were no old men in prison. Most died within a few years of being sent there. The conditions were deplorable, and for the most part, the guards didn't care who did what to whom.

It had taken some time, but Riggs found out what gave Louis Morgan so much power. It turned out he had shown up in the right place at just the right time, interrupting the warden engaged in a 'private party' with two inmates. That type of thing was to be expected in prison with no females around, but the warden was a married man, and the general public would not take kindly to such behavior. So, Louis' power held only as long as the warden stayed at the prison or didn't have Louis murdered.

As much as Louis no longer resembled a privileged gentleman when Riggs met him, Riggs had also changed. Hauling heavy baskets and bags of potatoes and rice had altered his physique. He had never been one for physical labor, something no one would ever know to look at him now. Deep frown lines creased his face, and he had aged more than the six years he had been there.

"You should be up for parole in a year," Louis said, finishing up the end of a cigarette.

"Does that mean the time is coming for me to take you to your nephew?" Louis wasn't due for parole, but he had said he could break out any time. His only goal was to kill Grayson, and after that, he didn't care what happened.

"Pretty much."

"As much as I would like to get even with him myself, I don't want to end up back here. So, as we agreed, I'll take you to where he is, and the rest will be up to you." Riggs hoisted another fifty-pound bag of flour onto his shoulder. Little white clouds puffed out from the seam.

"What makes you so sure he is still there?" Louis asked.

"He is. There's no place else for him to go."

"Yeah. That's what you keep tellin' me. I'm sure my mother is dead by now. Not that it matters. Tell me again about that sweet little mixed wife of my nephew. Might have to look her up after I'm done with him."

Riggs had repeatedly heard Louis' fantasies about what he would do to Grayson's wife. Personally, he wasn't one for such things and, after six years, was frankly tired of hearing about it. All he wanted was to get out of there, take Louis to the local village, make a ruckus so Morgan showed up, and then leave. Where he would go after that, he had no idea.

Perhaps change his name and start over somewhere; there were always jobs for cooks.

He'd had years to think. So many things he would have done differently, most of all being so hot-headed that his anger had gotten him caught. He would never be a respected man again, but he didn't have to be known as Samuel Riggs again, either. Sometimes he wondered what his sister Mary thought. He had just disappeared. He had never been a praying man, but had he been, one thing he might have prayed for would be that she never found out what had happened. It surprised him that he cared about it at all. But in some deeply hidden part of his heart, he did.

CHAPTER 3

The day had come to tell Lulnomia. The Great Entrance was filled to capacity as Pan began to speak.

"It is time for me to bring the Promised One here. He is pulling more and more power from the vortex, and his presence at Kthama will soon no longer be shielded from detection by those living at Zuenerth. When I return with him, he will live here as part of the community, but also, at times, he will live and train with Wrollonan'Tor and me. Also returning will be his brother Nootau and the six Sassen Guardians who were created at the time Kthama Minor was opened. Wrollonan'Tor and I will train them as well. I know I can count on you to welcome them all."

There was a murmur of excitement. When it died down, Wosot asked, "When will you leave?"

"Shortly. I will not be gone long, only enough to address the communities at Kthama and Kht'shWea.

And, of course, for their families to say their good-byes. Later, when An'Kru is ready, he will leave Lulnomia to fulfill his destiny, though I do not know how far off in the future that will be."

"Their quarters are ready, Guardian," Irisa interjected.

"Thank you, Overseer," Pan replied.

After she was done speaking, Pan remained for a while to answer any personal questions others might have. Naha and Moart'Tor approached her.

"I had hoped to return with you to Kthama," Moart'Tor remarked. "But I need to stay here with my mate."

"I understand," Pan replied.

Naha spoke up, "Moart'Tor told me about the Sassen female he met at Kayerm."

"Yes, Eitel," Pan confirmed.

"Would you please find out how she is doing?" Moart'Tor asked. "I have felt bad all this time about how I treated her."

"Of course," Pan agreed. "I certainly understand the need to address any lingering regrets about the past. I will find out and let her know you asked about her."

It was a quiet morning at the High Rocks. But not for long. Acaraho had just finished meeting with his

Circle of Counsel. As it was a beautiful day, they had met outside and were coming up one of the main paths to Kthama when there was a flash of light, and the Guardian Pan stood before them.

Mapiya was closest to where Pan was now standing. "Oh!" she gasped.

Acaraho immediately looked across at his mate.

"You have come to take An'Kru and Nootau to Lulnomia," Adia stated.

"Yes, and the six male Sassen Guardians as well."

"I knew the time was close," Adia said, "not only because An'Kru will be seven in three days, but also because even when only eleven of the Guardians are in his presence, all those nearby can feel a surge of energy."

Pan stepped forward to place a hand on Adia's shoulder. "I promise you all of them will be welcomed and will be safe and loved."

The Mothoc Guardian turned to Acaraho. "Adik'-Tar, I would like to address your community and then Haan's."

Acaraho nodded to High Protector Awan, who left to tell Haan of Pan's arrival and her request.

Soon, Awan returned with Haan and the Sassen High Protector, Qirrik.

"I can assemble our people quickly," Haan said, "if that is acceptable to you?"

"And then perhaps this evening you can meet

with the People of the High Rocks," Acaraho suggested.

"That is fine. Haan, please have all the Sassen Guardians assembled and let the males know they will be returning with me in three days. Tell them so they can say their goodbyes to their mates and offling. The same goes for your sons, Acaraho."

Acaraho turned to Awan, "Please dispatch a messenger to the Far High Hills and let Overseer Urilla Wuti know what is happening."

When they disbanded, Adia and Acaraho went to call their family together. Soon they were all assembled in the Healer's Quarters.

Acaraho told them about Pan's appearance. "Nootau and An'Kru will be leaving with Pan in three days, along with the male Sassen guardians."

Iella and Nootau slid closer together, and Nootau snaked his arm around his mate's back while she took his free hand in hers and clasped it tightly.

"Are you alright, Mother?" he asked.

"I have had years to prepare for this. I will miss you, of course. But I know Pan will not let anything happen to you, either of you. It is hard for me really to comprehend, though, that the next time I see you will perhaps be many years in the future. You will both be older; An'Kru will be grown."

"Do not worry about any of us, Nootau," Iella said. "Do what you have to do, and just come home safely."

"Even after all this time to prepare myself, it is still hard to think of leaving," Nootau said. "Even though I have known for so many years that I would be looking after and helping An'Kru."

"I will miss you, brother," Oh'Dar said to Nootau. "And so will the children, but the boys especially. You have played a huge role in their lives."

"We have not had time to talk to the offspring yet," Acaraho said. "We will after we leave here."

"The twins are old enough to understand this is something you must do," Oh'Dar added, "but I know they will grieve."

"The same with us," Acise said. "We will talk to our three as soon as possible. And, of course, Miss Vivian and Ben."

"How I wish Apricoria could control her ability to see the future."

"I know, Mother, but she cannot, any more than I can control what information I am given." Nootau sighed. "Nor can Haan, apparently."

"I am sure if Apricoria knew anything," added Acaraho, "the Overseer would have sent word."

Would she? Adia thought. *Depending on what Apricoria saw.* Adia recognized that fear, long subdued by An'Kru's visit so many years ago, was rising again.

Her memory returned to her first conversation with Pan, in the Corridor.

The air changed, suddenly tinged with exuberance. Adia felt almost lightheaded, something she had never before experienced in the Corridor. Then a figure, even larger than E'ranale, began to materialize in front of her. Had she been on Etera, Adia would have been afraid, but instead, she was intrigued and drawn to the essence taking form in front of her. It could only be Pan.

Adia waited silently, in awe. Pan smiled and said, "I am sorry my appearance here startles you."

"I am not really startled," Adia said, almost apologetic. "Perhaps. I am not sure. You are Pan."

"Yes."

"The last of the Mothoc Guardians."

"Yes," Pan nodded.

"Why have you brought me here?"

"I thought it was time we met. I know you have questions now that An'Kru has arrived."

Adia swallowed hard. "I am afraid I will fail him."

"Why?" Pan frowned. "Because he is different? This is not the first different offspring you will have raised."

"No. Well, yes. Because I feel he has a destiny to fulfill. And I am afraid I will not be up to giving him all he needs. That I will let him down."

"Every one of us has a destiny, and fear is always the enemy. Fear makes us doubt ourselves, doubt others, and doubt what we know. Right now, you are fearful of many things, but I assure you they are all illusions that you

have manufactured in your own mind. You know that it would not be given to you if you were not able to accomplish it."

"Yes," Adia admitted quietly. "Deep inside, I believe that."

"Then, when these fears surface, you must go deep inside. You have been guided. You will be guided. You are always guided. Even when things seem to be out of place, somewhere deep down, the Order of Functions is still engaged."

"But terrible things have happened. Painful things. How do I know tragedy will not befall An'Kru—due to my shortcomings?" Adia asked.

"Look to your left, Adia," Pan said, "and tell me what you see?"

"A row of locust trees, and beyond them, a field of the most vibrant and beautiful flowers I have ever seen."

"Past that," Pan said.

Adia looked around. "The horizon."

"And can you see what is beyond the horizon?"

"No."

"Your realm is filled with horizons. Because you are living in time, you have a limited view of events. You cannot see beyond what is happening, much as you cannot see beyond the horizon over there. You cannot see the interconnection that is always taking place beyond your comprehension and imagination. Whether you know it or not, things are unfolding as they should."

"What you do not see is already seen and compensated for by the Order of Functions," she continued.

Adia closed her eyes. "I will never understand this."

"You will. One day, when you stand here beside me forever, free from time, it will all make sense. Until then, you must learn to trust that which you cannot see. You must have—"

"Faith," Adia said. "My whole life seems to be a lesson about learning to have faith."

"It is so with everyone. That is part of your journey on Etera. We must trust what we cannot see, what we cannot understand. We must trust that no matter what, no matter how painful, how challenging, life is unfolding around us in the most beneficent way possible for our souls' paths."

Aponi, Nelairi, and An'Kru listened as their parents explained that the time had come, and the Guardian had arrived to take An'Kru and Nootau with her. Aponi and Nelairi asked the usual questions they had asked before, for which there were no answers. Where were they going? How long would they be gone? What would they do there? Acaraho and Adia assured them as best they could that An'Kru and Nootau would be protected and cared for.

Finally, An'Kru spoke, "Do not be afraid or have concerns for my brother and me. This is a part of our journey. I am happy that Nootau will be coming with us, though I know it makes it harder on everyone else."

Once again, Adia marveled at An'Kru's maturity. He spoke like an adult and had the insight of one far older than his seven years.

"Trust that we will return as soon as possible, but only when the time is right," he continued.

Nelairi took his hand. "I want to spend lots of time with you before you go, An'Kru."

"Of course! We can do whatever you want. You too, Aponi. All your favorite things!"

"And Nootau!" Aponi added. "But he will also want to be with Iella."

When they were done talking, Aponi and Nelairi left, though An'Kru stayed a moment longer. He walked over and stood very close in front of his parents. He took their hands.

"Mother, Father," he said. "Remember my visit to Mother years ago when I assured her that I must fulfill my destiny, walk the path that is laid out before me."

"You know about that?" Adia gasped. "How?"

"The Guardian told me. Through the years, she has visited with me many times in the Corridor."

"You never told us that," Acaraho said, his voice lowered.

"I did not want to constantly remind you that I

would be leaving. I wanted our focus to be on each moment, each day, and our time together."

Who is this soul? Adia thought. The Guardian had said An'Kru was a Guardian but also *something else*.

Then, becoming his true age suddenly, as sometimes happened, An'Kru threw his arms up, reaching as far as he could to embrace them both. "I love you so much." He was almost sobbing.

Adia's heart nearly broke. There are some things not even all the assurances in the world can assuage when the time comes to say goodbye to a beloved, even if only temporarily.

"I will be back before you know it." Then he released them from his embrace, turned, and left.

Acaraho pulled Adia into his embrace. There were no words to say; he simply held her close, and she melted into his arms. They stood together like that for some time.

Iella was trying to be strong for her mate. But inside, her heart was breaking. She tried discretely to wipe a tear from her cheek. "We have known for six years this day was coming. But somehow, that has not made it any easier."

"Nor for me, either." Nootau stroked her hair and then caressed her face.

"Perhaps, if Adia approves, I will return to the Far

High Hills and visit my parents for a while—after you leave, I mean."

"I think that is a good idea. Adia will fill in as Healer, and it will perhaps help her busy herself while she adjusts to our absence."

Iella sighed, "I know you need to spend time with your parents and your siblings before you leave. You must go ahead. We have our nights together."

Nootau leaned down, and she gladly accepted his kiss. "Alright, I will do that. But our nights belong only to us, as you said."

Haan gathered his community to tell them of the Guardian's return and remind them what it meant. The twelve Sassen Guardians were standing together in front of the crowd. Once he was done speaking, Pan appeared as if on cue.

The crowd gasped, and then nearly all turned to one another, excited at her arrival. The six male Guardians almost simultaneously clasped hands with their mates, who were standing with them, gathering their offling close. Despite their matching coats, Pan was easily identifiable because she towered over the Sassen Guardians.

"Greetings, people of Kht'shWea. You know by my standing before you that it is time to take the Promised One and his brother, as well as Thord,

Clah, Norir, Zok, Jokant, and Tarron, with me to Lulnomia." She moved closer to the six named before continuing.

"Lulnomia is a Mothoc community located far from here. It is to Lulnomia that the Ancients went when they left your ancestors thousands of years ago. Since then, the Mothoc have lived their lives there, just as you have done here."

"During their time there, the Promised One and the male Guardians will develop their powers. When the time is right, we will return, and the Promised One will open the path to Wrak-Ashwea. Until that time, know that your loved ones will be welcomed, protected, and loved."

Pan waited to see if anyone had questions. But if they did, nobody raised them. No doubt their silence was due partly to awe, partly to sadness over their community members leaving, and partly from a clash of other emotions.

As Pan was preparing to return to wherever she would be staying until it was time to leave, she remembered Moart'Tor's request. "Haan, is the female Eitel still here among you?"

"Yes, Guardian."

"Would you please introduce me to her?"

Haan quickly scanned the crowd and spotted Eitel, which was not difficult to do as her black coat was one of only a few. Qirrik saw her at the same time as Haan and went to retrieve her.

Eitel seemed to be transfixed, standing in front of Pan. Pan explained, "You knew Moart'Tor when he stayed at Kayerm, yes?"

"Yes. Quite a few of us here did, including my brother Naahb."

"He has asked about you and wanted me to find out how you are faring."

"Oh," Eitel stammered. "I am well." Then she added, "I think of him often, Guardian. I hope he has made a life for himself at—Lulnomia?"

"He has. He and his mate are expecting their first offling." Pan watched sadness come over Eitel's face.

"I see. I have not paired. I suppose it is silly of me, after all this time. I assume you can imagine— Well, I developed an affection for him that I was not able to shake until recently. I have now decided perhaps I am ready to be paired myself."

"I will tell him that. He will be glad to hear that you are moving forward into the future of your own making." Pan could see and feel that the news about Moart'Tor had indeed bothered the other female.

"Guardian, may I be excused now?" Eitel asked, her voice breaking just enough to be noticeable.

"Yes, of course." Eitel started to walk away, but Pan called after her.

"I think you should know that you were in Moart'Tor's heart for a long time. He had a true affection for you and often told me how much he regretted rebuffing you."

"Thank you for telling me, Guardian. Please tell him I am well and wish him and his mate all the best."

Off in the distance, Naahb was watching the conversation. He kept his eye on his sister and waited, hoping she would come directly to him. She did, and he put his arm around her shoulders and led her back inside Kayerm.

"Are you crying?" he asked as they walked.

"I am trying not to. How am I doing?" She attempted a smile.

"Failing terribly," he affectionately answered, tightening his arm around her shoulder to draw her closer.

"I think, as painful as that was, I needed it," she said. "I am ready to be paired, brother."

Naahb stopped. "That is great news. I mean, if it is true. Mother and Father will be excited because they have seen you pine for Moart'Tor through these years. They, like me, only want you to be happy."

"There is something I still want to do, and then I think I will be completely ready."

CHAPTER 4

If Visha was upset before that Kaisak had not even tried to find Moart'Tor, she was nearly beside herself now. Years had passed with no word of him and not even a hint of action on her mate's part. The hope that her firstborn son was still alive somewhere was nearly extinguished. But she still wanted to know either way.

Kaisak never spoke of Moart'Tor, only barely acknowledging when Visha brought him up. The seed of her resentment had grown, causing a widening rift between them. In the back of her mind, Visha came to believe that her mate had used Moart'Tor without regard for his well-being. She wondered if he would have done the same with the sons he had seeded. His promise to her, before they were paired, to love and raise Moart'Tor as his own now seemed hollow. A lie.

Try as she might not to mention it again, she

could not stop herself. One evening, while they were gathering wood for their evening fire, she spoke. "Kaisak, it has been years now. Do you never wonder what happened to Moart'Tor?"

"Since there is no way to know, I do not worry myself with speculation. I prefer to believe that he is well and living at Kayerm, perhaps even has a mate and offling."

Visha stopped placing sticks on the fire, her face contorted into an angry frown, "How can you possibly think that? How would that even be possible? Are you saying he is happily living mixed in with the Sassen? That is preposterous." She threw down the bundle in her hands.

"Would you prefer to think he is dead? Returned to the Great Spirit?"

Visha stormed over to her mate and slapped him hard across the face. "I prefer to think that his father might actually give a 'Rok about what happened to his son. But that's right, Moart'Tor is not your son is he? Is that it? *Is that the real truth about this?* That you used him for your own purposes? All the time he was growing up filling his head with your nonsense about his great mission to serve his people? Oh, why did I not see this before? You never cared for him, because he is not your son. He is Dak'Tor's, and you could never forget that."

Hearing the commotion, their grown sons came

over with their much younger brother. "What is going on?" scowled the oldest, Morvar'Nul.

Nofire'Nul, only slightly younger, broke in. "Everyone can hear you yelling at each other. What is it this time?"

At his brothers' raised voices, the youngest, Vollen'Nul, stepped back several paces.

"I do not care if you are grown or not; you will stop your disrespect," Kaisak started toward the two oldest. Morvar'Nul and Nofire'Nul backed up in time, leaving just enough space for Visha to step between them and her mate.

"Stop it! What are you doing?" She gestured wildly at Kaisak. "Have you lost your mind? Are you so filled with hatred that you do not even know who is the enemy and who is not? You would assault your own sons?"

Kaisak turned and rubbed his hand over his face, then over and behind the crown of his head.

"Vollen'Nul," she barked to their youngest, "go inside. You do not need to hear this."

"Mother, he will still be able to hear this. Everyone can hear you fighting," said Morvar'Nul.

"What do you want me to do, Visha?" Kaisak said as he turned around to face his mate again. "Send others after him? So they can suffer the same fate? Whatever that is. Tell me how that will help anything?"

Visha felt his gaze throwing daggers at her. "It is

probably too late now. But if you had not waited so long, maybe someone could have found him!"

"He is gone, Visha, "Kaisak bellowed. "You have to start accepting that. Either he got hurt and died, or got lost and starved to death, or he did find the Sassen, and they murdered him. Whatever it is, *he is not coming back*."

"Nooooo!" Her anguished cries filled the dark. "Nooooo. He is still alive; I know it. He is out there somewhere, no doubt wondering why we—you— never sent anyone to find him. To help him. At least to find out what happened. You betrayed him *and us*. And everyone else who ever trusted you to do what was right."

Visha rushed off into the dark, huge tears rolling down her cheeks.

Kaisak turned on his sons. "What are you looking at? Go find something else to do. There is no reason for you to stand there and soak up all this drama."

The three brothers dispersed.

"I think we should go after Mother," Nofire'Nul said. "I do not like her going off alone, sad in the dark."

"Not yet," his older brother disagreed. "We need to give her a little time. She is very upset."

"She has a right to be," said Nofire'Nul. "She is right. Father has not done anything to find Moart'Tor."

"I feel as if there is something we should do to

help her. She is truly heartbroken. Both over Moart'Tor and over Father's lack of concern about what happened to him."

Everyone at Zuenerth had heard the couple fighting. It was not uncommon for Kaisak and Visha to quarrel, but lately, the arguments had gotten louder and more intense. And now the sons were actively involved.

Dak'Tor and Iria had been preparing their own fire but stopped when they heard the raised voices. When it finally became quiet, Dak'Tor said with a clenched jaw, "Visha is right. Kaisak used Moart'Tor."

It was time. Pan stood with Nootau, An'Kru, and the six male Guardians. Having said their final farewells, those who were close to them stood by, including the Guardians' mates—except Eyota. She had volunteered to stay away so all twelve would not be with An'Kru, even on this last occasion.

"I leave now with your loved ones. Lean into your faith that all is well."

"Wait!" Adia called out and rushed toward Pan. "Wait, please."

The Guardian looked down at the Healer, who could see only deep compassion when their gazes met.

"What do you need?" Pan asked.

"I know you will protect him. I know it. But part of me is now scared at this last moment. Please, I need a promise. A promise."

"Ask it then," Pan answered.

"Promise me, you will never leave An'Kru and Nootau at Lulnomia without you. Promise me that, please, Guardian. Promise me that until it is time for them to return here, you will always be with them at Lulnomia or anywhere else they might go."

"I know how hard this is for you. There was a time when I, too, was separated from my loved ones. I know a mother's heart is never truly eased when it comes to her offlings' welfare. I also know you trust me. But if you need a promise, here it is. I promise you, Adia. I will stay with your sons at all times until it is time for them to return safely to you."

Adia bent her head and covered her face with her hands. "Thank you," she quietly said.

Acaraho stepped forward and led his mate back to the rest of their family, who drew close in an attempt to comfort her.

Pan waited a moment to see if anyone else wanted to ask or say anything. When no one did, she raised her hand and said, "We will leave you now.

Until the Order of Functions, in its infinite orchestration of our realm, reunites us."

This time there was a bright flash of light, and Pan, the six male Guardians, Nootau, and An'Kru were gone.

The others stood staring at the empty space as if half thinking they might reappear. Eventually, they dispersed, talking among themselves and comforting each other. No matter how much faith fills a heart, a loved one is still missed when no longer in the fold.

Almost within the same instant, Pan and her charges appeared in front of Lulnomia. Just as with Moart'-Tor, she gave them a moment to take in the stunning surroundings. The glistening snow-covered mountains rising to meet the sky, the deep green of the firs blanketing the landscape. And there was Lulnomia's entrance, flanked by towering evergreens, beckoning them to enter.

Just as with Moart'Tor's arrival, the Great Entrance was empty. Those with Pan looked around, their gazes running over the white stone floors, the iridescent snow crystals sparkling in the light that broke through the entrance, and the high ceiling, frozen and blanketed with ice.

Suddenly a deep resounding voice broke the

silence. "I am Wrollonan'Tor, Guardian of the Ancients. Welcome to Lulnomia."

He appeared before them.

Against his will, Nootau gasped. It was a behemoth, covered in the same silver-white coat as An'Kru and all the Guardians, though larger even than Pan. More muscular, broader. It would be impossible to imagine anyone more powerful.

Nootau instinctively reached out and pulled An'Kru behind him.

"Do not be alarmed. I realize my size is intimidating." The giant let out a quiet chuckle. "It is alright, Nootau, son of Khon'Tor, son of Acaraho, son of the Healer, Adia. No harm will come to any of you here."

Nootau felt An'Kru take his hand and step forward. "It really is fine, brother." An'Kru's voice was reassuring, and Nootau felt the offspring gently tug him forward toward the one named Wrollonan'Tor.

"Where are we—" Nootau asked.

"This is Lulnomia. This is the home of the Mothoc, almost all those who still walk Etera."

Feeling the frigid air, Nootau wrapped his arms around his body. Just as he did so, a very elderly female stepped into the room.

"Here," she said, "I had these prepared for you." She handed Nootau a heavy wrap made of furred hide and a smaller one to An'Kru. "I am Irisa. I am Wrollonan'Tor's daughter and Overseer of Lulnomia."

She was old. Not frail, but Nootau could see the age upon her. Not only on her body but also in her eyes. As if she had lived a long time and had enough of this world.

"You are perceptive," she said to him. "Yes, I am old. Very old. The oldest one alive on Etera, other than my father. Now that I have seen the Promised One, soon I will return to the Great Spirit."

Irisa turned her eyes to An'Kru, who left Nootau's side. She bent down to address him. "I waited for you."

"I am happy you did, but it is not yet time for you to leave; we have only just met. It will not be long, though, I promise."

The others listened, amazed at how An'Kru spoke. He was not even halfway grown, yet he spoke with authority and wisdom.

Irisa nodded to An'Kru and turned back to the others.

"We are ready for you all," she said. "The community is anxious to meet you."

Wrollonan'Tor then turned to the six Sassen Guardians. He called them by name. "Thord, Clah, Norir, Zok, Kant, Tarron, welcome. In a moment, the people of Lulnomia will appear. At present, you are cloaked from their awareness, as I wanted to have a moment alone with you before you are revealed to the community. In time, you will come to know many of them well. And before long, you will visit me in my realm, and the Guardian Pan and I will continue your training."

Nootau remembered someone saying that, for some time, Pan had been training the six male Guardians in the Corridor.

In the next instant, a crowd of Mothoc materialized in the Great Entrance. This time Nootau caught himself before he gasped out loud. If a group of Sassen was intimidating, a group of Mothoc was exponentially so. Nootau noticed that even the six Sassen Guardians flinched at being surrounded by a multitude of those so much larger than they were.

Clash whispered to Thord, "Now I understand how the Akassa sometimes feel when they are with us!"

"Unnerving, to say the least," Thord whispered back.

A chill went up Nootau's spine as, taking in the size of the Mothoc in juxtaposition to the Sassen, he realized for the first time the possibility of the rebel Mothoc succeeding in destroying both his people and Haan's. *If* they had the numbers and *if* enough of them attacked at once. It was not only that the Mothoc were so much larger than the Sassen; the difference was also in their physical strength. For a moment, he wondered, if it came to that, would the Mothoc at Lulnomia intervene to save the People and the Sassen? Would Mothoc ever rise against Mothoc?

For a moment, in his mind's eye, Nootau saw

such a battle. The clashing of powerful claws and glistening canines, terrorizing howls and growls scattering wildlife far and wide. Blood splattering everywhere. Huge bodies crashing into the landscape, uprooting and felling entire groves of trees with their impact. In the background, females viciously fighting for the lives of their offling. Wailings of grief, the moans of the wounded, and the stench of blood filling the air.

With a shudder, he tried to clear his mind of the carnage. Was it just his imagination? Was this a vision? He couldn't tell, but immediately he prayed to the Great Spirit for such a future never to come about.

Wrollonan'Tor addressed the crowd. "Behold, the prophecy is true. The Promised One stands before you."

As if on cue, An'Kru stepped toward the crowd. Nootau watched the Mothoc's reaction as their eyes ran up and down the tiny Akassa male. The six white Sassen Guardians standing behind him all fell to one knee and bowed their heads. Then, Thord rose, raised a hand upward, and declared, "An'Kru is the One Promised. He is the Seventh of the Six, the one who has come to open the path to Wrak-Ashwea."

"Arise, Guardians," Wrollonan'Tor said. "Let our history record and our hearts remember that this is the day the Promised One came to Lulnomia."

Pan accompanied Irisa to take their guests to their quarters. As Nootau and An'Kru were the only Akassa there, Irisa had arranged for them to share large living quarters. Next to them were the six Sassen Guardians, their rooms flanking those of Nootau and An'Kru. If she had a concern, it was for Nootau. Seeing him standing next to An'Kru, seeing how small and frail the Akassa were compared to everyone at Lulnomia, she worried that this might be harder for him than she had anticipated. After all, An'Kru and the six Sassen Guardians had years of training ahead of them, but how would Nootau's time here be spent?

After Pan had left Irisa to further settle their guests, she saw Moart'Tor approaching her.

"Guardian, I am glad you have returned."

"How is Naha? Has she delivered your offling?"

"Not yet, but it will be soon. All seems to be going well. The Promised One—even though you told me he is an Akassa, it still shocked me. He definitely has a Guardian's coloring. Is his brother then, the one named Nootau, more like the other Akassa?"

"Yes," Pan answered.

"Did you learn anything of Eitel?"

"I did speak with her. She spoke of you as you did of her—that she also felt affection for you.

When I told her you had paired, she said she has finally come to a point where she is ready to pair, too."

"*Finally*?"

"I do not mean to make you feel worse than you do, but yes. Finally. It has taken her this long to put the memory of you behind her."

"I see. I am glad to hear she is now ready to move forward."

Just then, Jhotin, one of the Healer Helpers, came running up to Moart'Tor. "Excuse me, Guardian. Moart'Tor, your mate is having your offling."

"Go!" Pan said, smiling.

Moart'Tor waited outside with Naha's father. Her mother was in with Naha and the Healers, Tyria, and Pagara. Before too long, Moart'Tor heard an offling's cry, after which Lai came out and told him he had a healthy son.

"There were no problems and no complications. And your son is healthy and strong, as you can hear!" She led Moart'Tor in to see his mate and son.

"He has your markings—well, most of them at this moment," Lai said.

The senior Healer, Pagara, was now one of the elders, having lived since the time of Straf'Tor. As Moart'Tor came in, they all stepped back to give him room beside his mate and their newling.

"You have a son," Naha was grinning from ear to ear.

"I see that. He is perfect. And how are you feeling?"

"Tired. But happy. I am glad you did not go with Pan," Naha admitted.

"I would not leave you alone waiting to give birth. Not if I could help it." Moart'Tor peeked down at the bundle in his mate's arms.

"Look," Naha pulled the wrap back to show her mate his son. Two little eyes opened just enough for Moart'Tor to see them. They were a beautiful brown, just like his mother's. Naha pulled the wrap back a little further. "See his hair? It is going to be silver, like yours. At least on his head, I am not yet sure about the rest."

"He is perfect, no matter his coloring. Have you named him?"

"I was thinking Yoomee'Tor," Naha said, looking at Moart'Tor for approval.

Moart'Tor blinked. His mouth opened just a bit and froze there. It was customary for the father to approve of the mother's name choices. But this—

He turned to look at the others in the room and saw blank expressions on their faces.

Just then, Naha burst out laughing. "I am kidding! No, how about Akoth'Tor."

Everyone in the room, including Moart'Tor, broke out laughing. Naha's father came up and slapped him on the back, "Now you are starting to find out who you are really paired to."

Her mother was also still laughing at her daughter's teasing.

Moart'Tor finally stopped smiling and said to his mate, "That is a good name. I approve of your choice."

"She will be going home in the morning. I want her here tonight to help her, so she gets a full night's sleep," said Pagara. "So you also please try to sleep well tonight."

Moart'Tor kissed Naha and brushed the top of Akoth'Tor's head, and left. By the time he got to their living quarters, he saw that, as was tradition, the older females had brought in extra food and niceties to help Nala through the first days of adjusting to having an offling. It was one of the few times that others entered another's living quarters without permission, as it was customary to provide gifts to the new parents.

"I have a son," Moart'Tor said out loud. Then louder, "I have a son!" He dropped to his knees, the rock floor a harsh surface to land on, but he didn't care. "Thank you, Great Spirit. Thank you for making a way to bring me out of my ignorance so I could inherit such great blessings as you have showered on me since I left Zuenerth. I believed having a mate and family was out of reach, yet here I am today, living a life I could never have imagined."

He went on to pray for his loved ones and others around him, for Pan, Irisa, and a multitude more. For the six Sassen Guardians, the Promised One, and the Akassa.

Then in closing, he bowed his head, "Let me better hear your voice so I may better serve you and Etera."

Pan walked through Lulnomia, hoping to run into Nootau. She did find Irisa and asked where the Akassa was. "He is with An'Kru and your mate. Rohm'Mok is giving them a tour of Lulnomia."

Pan smiled; that was so like her mate, to be thoughtful of others. She took a deep breath and relaxed. Oddly she had no qualms about An'Kru finding his place; it was more that his place had found him. But Nootau.

"Where will I find them?" Pan asked.

"A moment ago, they were in the Great Chamber."

"Oh, I did not think about them being hungry. And the Sassen Guardians?"

"After your mate told me he was going to show An'Kru and Nootau around, I did the same with the Sassen. I explained the daily routines, meal times, and how the tunnels are divided between the different communities. I believe they will be fine. To let them first get used to being here, Father will not call them for a few days."

"Thank you, dear friend. I am going to find my mate and his charges."

The three of them were eating. Pan said hello and, at his prompting, sat down next to Rohm'Mok. She asked how they were doing.

"I thought Kthama was big," Nootau exclaimed. "I am not sure I can comprehend the size of Lulnomia."

"Yes, and there are areas that, even in all this time, we have not inhabited. We have not needed to. There are tunnels and branches that snake deep within the mountain range. We have explored many of them, but we are not sure how far they reach or where they surface. It just has not been something that was an issue. We have them blocked off, for now, to ensure no one gets lost."

Nootau said, "I see the same markings as are on our tunnels. It is reassuring. I am glad I can understand them."

"Our roots are your roots, so it is understandable," Rohm'Mok added.

An'Kru just sat silently listening with a contented look on his face.

Nootau put his hand on his brother's shoulder and playfully jostled him. "He does not talk unless he has something noteworthy to say," he teased.

"You talk enough for both of us." An'Kru grinned at his big brother.

Pan and Rohm'Mok smiled at seeing the two brothers teasing each other. At that moment, An'Kru seemed an ordinary offling, yet he was anything but.

"I have been pelting Nootau with a thousand questions, I am afraid," Rohm'Mok said. "About the High Rocks and the Akassa communities. The Sassen."

Pan made a steeple with her fingers and put it briefly to her lips. "That gives me an idea. Nootau, our people no longer know anything of the Akassa or the Sassen, although our older members grieved for a long time over leaving them. Would you be willing to teach those who are interested in them? Share your life experiences, perhaps?"

"I would be glad to," Nootau answered.

Pan was happy to see another smile on his face. "Wrollonan'Tor would like you to attend some of the training the Sassen Guardians and An'Kru will be going through," she added.

"Why? I mean, I would be glad to, but I have no special abilities. Well, sometimes information comes to me out of nowhere, but I cannot control it."

"You studied with Urilla Wuti, the Akassa Overseer, for some time, did you not?"

"Yes. She believed I might have some dormant Healer abilities."

"I believe you do." Then Pan leaned forward and

looked him in the eye. "It is not a mistake that you are here, Nootau."

Nootau closed his eyes and nodded. She could feel relief spreading through him.

An'Kru reached out and touched his brother. "I am glad you are with me."

Once again, An'Kru seemed to be only a normal offling, not the Promised One whose coming would open the path to the Age of Light. Pan and her mate exchanged a quick glance, smiling again at the heart-warming demonstration of love between the two brothers.

CHAPTER 5

"What are we going to do," Nofire'Nul asked his older brother.

"Do? About what? Moart'Tor, or Mother and Father quarreling?" Morvar'Nul asked.

"All of it. We cannot just continue to do nothing. Unless something changes, I fear Mother will leave him."

"That does not happen."

"It has happened before," said Nofire'Nul. "I have heard others speak of it. And they are so angry with each other now, more than I have ever seen before."

"What do you suggest we do, brother? I do not see how we can help them."

"We could try to find Moart'Tor."

"What? And what good would that do? We have no idea where he is. Or how to get to Kayerm, if he even made it that far."

"Useaves knows where Kayerm is."

"That old Healer. No, thank you, I do not trust her."

"Then Gard. He knows. He is the one who told Moart'Tor how to find Kayerm," Nofire'Nul persisted.

"I do not think it is a good idea," Morvar'Nul said, shaking his head.

"But what if we found him? Or at least found out what happened to him?"

"Father would be so angry."

"Father is always angry. We are adults now; he does not control us. And I think it would mean a lot to Mother that we tried."

"You are probably right about that, assuming we come back alive."

"When did you become so cautious? You are the oldest; I thought you would be all for this."

Morvar'Nul told his brother to sit down, pointing to a nearby boulder. "I am the oldest, and because of that, I have to look out for you. And Vollen'Nul, too. If anything happened to you, it would be my fault."

"We will be together, and we can cloak."

"We cannot cloak ourselves from the other Mothoc."

"But we can from the Akassa and the Sassen. What if we were to find Moart'Tor?! And what if we discovered where Kthama is? We would be such heroes that Father could not afford to be angry with us."

Morvar'Nul let out a long sigh. "Let me think

about it. There are two of us. And Father has always claimed that Mothoc will never rise against Mothoc. It is dangerous, but then many of the most worthwhile endeavors are."

"Think of how happy Mama would be. And surely, for our heroism, we would be granted females!"

Morvar'Nul shook his head, smiling at his brother. "I admire your courage. And your spunk. As I said, let me think about it. But if we do this, we cannot tell anyone, and Mother will worry herself sick about what happened to us."

"We can tell Gard, but make him swear not to tell them until we are far along the way. Mother will still worry, but at least she will know where we went."

"I cannot believe I am even considering this," Morvar'Nul said, then noticed the huge smile turning up the corners of his younger brother's mouth.

Over the next few weeks, they talked in secret about their plan. They were confident that if Moart'Tor had found Kayerm, they would also be able to. And if nothing else, they could observe the Sassen at Kayerm, though they would have to be watchful to hide from the Mothoc. The odds were that they would be discovered, but they were confident they would not be harmed. No matter what anyone else thought, from the stories the elders told of the Sacred Laws and their adherence to them, neither of the two brothers believed either the Sassen, the Akassa, or the other Mothoc would have harmed their oldest brother.

Their parents' fighting continued, and the young males heard their mother telling their father he had to sleep elsewhere. And so Kaisak set up another sleeping area. They hardly spoke to each other, which in some ways was as worrisome as the arguing.

"It is time," Morvar'Nul said. "Time for us to speak with Gard."

Gard listened patiently. When they had finished, he said, "Are you both mad?"

Both brothers looked at each other, their mouths agape. "No, we are not mad!" Morvar'Nul objected. "Someone has to do something. You have heard our parents arguing."

"Not lately, and the silence has been a relief," Gard answered.

"That is because they are no longer speaking to each other. If we do not do something, I cannot even guess what will happen next. We need our parents, and Zuenerth needs an Adik'Tar. If it is not our father, then who would it fall to?"

Gard pursed his lips. "Most likely you."

"I am not ready to lead Zuenerth," Morvar'Nul objected.

"You really do not believe your mother and father are going to come to blows with each other, do you?" Gard asked.

"We do not know what to think," Nofire'Nul interjected. "Please help us. We have at least to try and find Moart'Tor."

Gard shook his head. "Against my better judgment, I will help you. I will tell you what I told Moart'Tor, including my best advice on how to proceed. I agree with you that if he did find Kayerm, no harm would have come to him. So it only leaves the possibilities that he is still there and has somehow made a life for himself among the Mothoc —or that he never reached them."

"Why did we not think of that?" Nofire'Nul said. "There are Mothoc there as well as the Sassen. Mothoc females. Perhaps he took a mate. Perhaps he has a family now and found peace and happiness. Mother fears the worst became of him, but I never heard her speculate that he might not have returned because he made a life for himself there."

Over the next few days, Gard told them everything he had told their older brother. He drew in the dirt the path he had drawn for Moart'Tor. Though there was no magnetic stream leading directly to Kayerm, he pointed out the magnetic swells that would serve as markers to tell them they were on the right path. He explained about the patterns in the stars and landmarks to watch for, including the huge Oak tree that had once towered over the meadow adjacent to Kayerm. He told them about and described the Others. Mostly, he taught them to quiet their minds and listen to the guidance within, as his mother, Useaves, had taught him long ago —though, to Gard's discredit, he rarely took her advice.

"You promise that for as long as you can hold out, you will not tell our parents where we have gone?"

"I am taking a huge risk for you. Your father may well be very angry with me. As may your mother."

"Tell them we were going to do this anyway. That you helped us, against your better judgment, to give us the best chance at success," Nofire'Nul suggested.

"That would certainly be the truth. If I were younger, and my moth— If I were younger, I might even have gone with you."

"We will leave tonight after everyone has settled in," Morvar'Nul declared.

"May the Great Spirit guide and protect you both."

The fighting between Visha and Kaisak started up again once Visha discovered Morvar'Nul and Nofire'Nul were gone. Gard waited to pick his moment to approach them, wanting to give their sons as much time as possible to get away. He considered not confessing as he secretly enjoyed Kaisak's displeasure—but he knew Visha, being their mother, was suffering over not knowing anything, and he had made a promise.

The community was on fire, speculating what had become of them. The Mothoc had no natural enemies other than overgrown Sarius Snakes. The stories of what might have happened to them took on a life of their own. Some said they ran off because of their parent's fighting. Others said that the Guardian had taken them, though no one had a good reason for why she would do that. Kaisak sent search parties out, looking along the edges of the far canyons to see if they had perhaps slipped and fallen to their deaths. They searched for days, then weeks, until finally, Gard felt it was time to tell Visha and Kaisak.

"I have information for you about your missing sons," he said.

"What? Have you seen them? What do you know?" Visha demanded.

"Before I tell you, you must promise to wait until I finish before you speak."

"I promise," Visha immediately said. When Kaisak said nothing, Visha glared at him. "Promise Kaisak. Promise you will hear him out."

Reluctantly, Kaisak snarled, "I promise."

"You must hear me clearly. I did not want to help

them. But if I did not, the odds of their survival would greatly have been reduced. And they were going to do it anyway, with or without my help."

"Do what? What have they done?" Kaisak demanded

"Did you hear me, Kaisak?" Gard stared at their Leader. "Because if you blame me for this in any way, then I am done talking here and now."

Visha pleaded for him to continue. "We will not blame you, Gard, I promise."

"Your two sons have set out to find Moart'Tor, or to find out what happened to him."

"What?" Visha's eyes widened. "They have gone to Kayerm?"

"Yes. They made me promise not to tell you until they were well on their way. They did it for you, Visha. They did it because they could no longer bear your suffering and anguish. They did it because they believe that whatever they find out, no matter the outcome, it will help you to know. Even if it is bad news."

"Foolishness," Kaisak scoffed. He stormed about. "Now I have lost all of my sons except Vollen'Nul. At least they had enough sense not to take him."

"Morvar'Nul would not have let him go. He is protective of his brothers, all of them. He will not let any harm come to Nofire'Nul. And he is protective of you, Visha. They did this out of concern for your welfare."

Gard looked sternly at both Visha and Kaisak. "And for your relationship."

"Explain to me where they have gone; tell me what you told them, and I will send others after them," Kaisak barked.

"You would send others after them, but not Moart'Tor?" Visha raised her voice, "Did I just hear you say that? After all the years I begged you to do just that. And your excuse was always that it would do no good to send others to their deaths?"

Kaisak fell silent, knowing he had just made a fatal error. Perhaps literally.

"I hate you. I am sorry I ever paired with you. No matter what happens, I will never let you return to my bed. You have failed our sons, including Moart'-Tor, and you have failed me. And no doubt also the rest of Zuenerth."

Then she turned to Gard. "Thank you for telling us. And thank you for helping them. I believe you; they would have gone anyway. You have given them their best chance of returning safely home—with or without Moart'Tor." She stormed off, but Kaisak called after her.

"Where are you going?"

"The rest of the community deserves to know where Moart'Tor and Nofire'Nul have gone. And what kind of person you really are."

Dak'Tor was shocked. Not that the two brothers had set out after Moart'Tor, but that Visha had finally had it with Kaisak. It was obvious from her state that it was over between them. What that would do to Kaisak's position as Adik'Tar, Dak'Tor did not know. Not that he would step down, but it would seriously change how the people felt about him.

When they were alone, Iria said to him, "I am glad Morvar'Nul and Nofire'Nul left to try and find Moart'Tor. Even though they are grown, as a mother, I can imagine how worried Visha is."

"Yes. I pray they find him and return safely."

"Perhaps now others' view of Kaisak may change. Perhaps the community will lose faith in him, and his influence over them will lose its power."

"And in turn, you are hoping that their hatred of the Akassa and Sassen may also soften?"

"I believe it is possible," acknowledged Iria. "Even though it has been preached to them for thousands of years, we do not know how many really embrace it. They could be pretending as we have been. Or perhaps they have grown tired of so much hatred. So I can hope."

Their daughter was done nursing, so Iria set her in her nest, pulling the little hide wrap up around her, more for comfort than warmth.

"I think tomorrow I will try to talk to the others and get their thoughts about this," Dak'Tor said.

Iria knew that by the others, he meant those in their inner circle who secretly believed as they did that the Akassa and Sassen were not abominations.

As Dak'Tor settled in to sleep, he thought of his sister Pan. *Where are you?* He wished he could tell her how sorry he was for what he had done. Could she ever forgive him?

CHAPTER 6

The visitors stood before Wrollonan'Tor, who had Irisa and Pan at his side. "Relax, please," he said. "I will give you a moment to look around."

They were still recovering from the walk to where they were now standing. Down one of the paths leading away from Lulnomia, through the point where they felt a shift and the colors around them became more vibrant, deeper. Then to the towering rock wall and the entrance to the winding tunnel, finally coming to where they now stood, in the center of a great chamber.

They look around, taking in the smooth walls and the layer of dust beneath their feet. The ceiling towered above, though it was not as high as Lulnomia's.

Wrollonan'Tor's sonorous voice filled the chamber. "Welcome to my world."

Then, everything changed again. Every one of them startled as the ancient Guardian appeared.

"I have removed a level of cloaking. The deeper levels of my true nature are still hidden from you, though, so you will not be overwhelmed by my presence."

Nootau felt a wave of something pass through him. He was suddenly aware of the timelessness emanating from Wrollonan'Tor. Timelessness on an unfathomable scale. His gaze met that of the huge Guardian, and it was as if, for a brief moment, he and Wrollonan'Tor were one. He looked at the others and saw the same expression on their faces that he imagined was on his—except for An'Kru, who seemed to be as at home here as he was at Kthama.

Wrollonan'Tor went on to tell them what, so long ago, he had explained to Pan. About his existence there and how the Mothoc had been led to believe he had died. About when the mantle had passed to Pan's father, Moc'Tor. The ancient Guardian explained how this place had been created from his own essence according to his will and that, in time, they would all be able to do the same.

'Yes, Nootau, even you, although not to the same extent, as the concentration of Aezaitera in your blood is far less than that of the Promised One and the Sassen Guardians. Let me explain further. You may sit if you wish."

Nootau looked behind him, and a row of boulders appeared out of thin air.

"There is only one power, and it is positive, loving, beneficent. The creative force of the Great Spirit is present in every aspect of Etera. Even inanimate objects contain it. The life force, the Aezaitera, is only positive, and it encompasses both the male and the female traits.

"Etera is alive. Everything is alive because everything that exists is created from the living force of the One-Who-Is-Three. Even objects like rocks have the life-force in them. Everything in existence is made up of the creative life-force, though not everything, a rock, for example, has consciousness or awareness. And this is where the confusion lies, because when you say something is alive, what you mean is that you perceive it to have some level of awareness. But I digress. All of creation is engaged in the dance of life, whether we are aware of it or not.

"The three aspects of the Great Spirit work together in this ongoing creative act. The Great Heart is the creative force, love, from which everything is formed. The Great Mind is the unfathomable intellect that effortlessly thinks everything into existence in infinite combinations of complexity and order. Through the Great Will, the loving, creative force of the Great Heart and the exquisite design of the Great Mind's creation is continuously called into being.

"The Great Spirit has given us free will. The actions and even intentions of our free will are soul movements. The life force within each of us, the active male aspect of our soul movements, is received by the receptive feminine aspect of our existence and impacts our reality.

"We all have the creative life force within us, so we all have the ability to affect this realm through the actions of our free will, but also through our soul movements.

"The fact that Etera's realm is slow to respond to our influence has both good and bad aspects. How devastating would it be if our angry reactions and our desire for revenge could manifest themselves so quickly? On the other hand, we sometimes lose faith because our prayers do not immediately bring us results. So it is a double-edged blade. But understanding it is the first step to being able to control and increase our impact on our reality."

Wrollonan'Tor stopped and looked at each of them. Pan had already taught much of this to the six Guardians during their meetings in the Corridor. But repetition was a cornerstone of learning, and Nootau and An'Kru had not yet heard it.

"I think this is perhaps enough for today. Small steps are best. Irisa will take you back to Lulnomia, and we will meet here again tomorrow when I shall show you the training ground we will be working on."

On the walk back, Nootau asked Irisa, "Will I be able to learn this? I felt out of place there with the others. I came to be here with An'Kru and look after him. But he is handling it far better than any of us."

"Like most of us, you are blind to our own gifts. But to answer your question, yes, you will be able to learn what my father teaches you. Not to the extent of the Sassen Guardians or An'Kru, but I believe you will surprise yourself in the end. After we get back to Lulnomia, I will take you to Pan and let her explain more."

Irisa could feel that Pan was at the Healer's Cove. As she led Nootau up to it, he asked, "What is this place? It is so beautiful, and it feels sacred."

"This is the Healer's Cove," Irisa explained. "It is where the Healers and others of us come to commune with the Great Spirit and seek the Great Mother's will."

"There was one at Kthama. It concealed the entrance to Kht'shWea."

"Yes. I believe your Healers now go to the Guardian's Meadow above Kthama."

Pan turned around, having sensed they were on their way.

"We have just come from the first meeting with my father," Irisa said.

"Ah, I remember mine well," Pan smiled. "Over-whelming, to be sure."

"It certainly was," Nootau agreed.

"Nootau said he felt out of place there," continued Irisa. "As if he did not belong with the others my father will be training."

"I see," Pan said. "Come, Nootau, walk with me."

Irisa left them together.

"It is true that with all the training possible," began Pan, "your abilities will not equal those of the others. That is because the Aezaitera, the creative life force, is less concentrated in your blood—in the blood of all the Akassa except for An'Kru. It is a result of interbreeding with the Brothers. But the Aezaitera is there nonetheless, and you can learn to make the most of what you do have. I understand that you feel out of place, but remember, you are not here by acci-dent. You belong here as much as any of them.

"Do you believe me?" She caught up his gaze in hers.

"Yes, I believe you. However, I have to work on accepting it."

"In time, you will see. Now let me amend my statement. I said the Aezaitera is less concentrated in all the Akassa—all the Akassa except An'Kru. I once said that An'Kru is an Akassa Guardian—yes, but he is also *something more.* None of us knows his true abilities. The one who might have the truest idea would be Wrollonan'Tor, who was trained by An'Kru."

Nootau frowned and shook his head quickly. "Wait. An'Kru trained Wrollonan'Tor? This An'Kru?"

"Well, I trained An'Kru. And he trained Wrollonan'Tor."

"I am not going to pretend to understand how that is possible, but if you trained An'Kru, and An'Kru trained Wrollonan'Tor, how can Wrollonan'Tor be more powerful than you?"

"To understand this, you have to understand the timelessness of the Corridor. An'Kru visited you in the Corridor once, did he not?"

"Yes. He told me to let go of my fears of failing the Great Spirit."

"And he also told you your heart is pure—one of the purest ever. And he said it would guide you. But he did not explain the Corridor to you, so let me. In the Corridor, there is no change. Everything that was, or will be, already is. Here on Etera, we are living in the realm of change and affect. Our decisions affect our path, and the effects of our path affect us. We can only learn and grow in this realm where there is change—the impact of our free will and soul movements on the creative force here. But in the Corridor, there is no change."

Little did Nootau know that his mother had this

same conversation with E'ranale many years prior and had felt the same confusion.

"How can everything that has ever happened, or will happen, or whatever you said, all exist at once? If that is true, how can there be any order here? How does any separate moment exist?" Adia had asked.

"On Etera, if you are in your quarters and you leave to go to the common eating area, your living quarters still exist. They are still there; you are simply not experiencing them. That is what it is here. Everything exists at once, but you do not notice unless you focus your attention on it, and then you can, so to speak, enter that aspect of reality." With that, E'ranale motioned, and instead of the solitary magnolia tree, an entire grove appeared instantly.

"There is no past, no future; there is only now. This is also true in your realm, though because of change, you believe time is passing. Here there is no change, so no time passes. Everything always is. Your focus, your soul's deepest intention, and the next step on your journey create what slice of it you experience."

"So," finished Pan, "everything An'Kru learned is available to him in the Corridor. Only he seems to have brought some of it with him into this life, which I admit perplexes me."

"Is that why he seems so—adult?" Nootau asked.

"Possibly. At least, that is what I suspect. I do not know what the true extent of his abilities here will be."

"So, then, that is how An'Kru can appear as an adult in the Corridor," continued Nootau. "Because everything he ever was, is, or will be, exists at the same time, or, in a time of no time?"

"Yes. And it is how he could train Wrollonan'Tor with abilities that surpassed what I have. There are truths that, while we are on Etera, are beyond the ability of our minds to comprehend. That is where faith comes in. Faith takes us beyond what we see, hear, feel, or experience, beyond what our limited minds can comprehend—if we learn to trust it."

"So, I need to stop trying to understand it and accept what you tell me," Nootau said.

"Finding that place of acceptance, of trust in the Great Spirit and the Order of Functions, as well as letting go of the mind's need to understand, is the first step on your journey here. Congratulations, Nootau."

Training resumed the next day after they had all rested.

"Let me introduce you to my world." Wrollonan'Tor led them down one of the dark tunnels a fair distance. Finally, a light broke through at the far end. As they stepped through the opening, they found themselves back outdoors. It looked like Etera, the same kind of landscape, sky, trees, and even a lake—only more vibrant and alive. A deer poked her head out from the edge of a grove of trees.

"Are we in the Corridor?" Thord asked.

"No. We are still on Etera, only in a world of my creation. Remember, I explained that the Aezaitera is the creative power of the Great Spirit. I have spent much time connecting with it, and as a result, I, as well as Pan, have the ability to mold this level in any way I desire."

"Level?" Clah asked.

Wrollonan'Tor went on to explain vibrations and levels of existence, including how the Mothoc and Sassen could cloak themselves by shifting the vibration around them. "Your cloaking ability is the same concept. You change the vibration and extend the viewer's visual field, as if bending reality around you, so you become invisible."

The season in Wrollonan'Tor's world was spring. Then, to demonstrate, in an instant, it was fall. The green leaves had turned into a multitude of rich colors, the bright flowers of spring were replaced with tall brown grasses, and the bushes were loaded with fall berries. The temperature had dropped, and the deer's coat had changed from caramel to dark grey. Then, Wrollonan'Tor changed everything back to spring.

The six Guardians turned to each other in wonder. One of them, Clah, left the other five and stood next to Nootau. Clah's mate was Eyota, Adia's friend, and he wanted to ease Nootau's journey here as much as he could.

"In time, you will also learn to control the creative matter here, as I do. As Pan does," Wrollonan'Tor explained further.

"And back on Etera?" Tarron asked.

"Not to this extent, no. But what you learn here will serve you there in other ways, although it will not be quite so remarkable as this."

"What is that over there?" Nootau pointed.

In the next moment, Pan was standing next to them. "That is my home when I am here."

"May we see it?" Nootau asked.

"Of course!" Pan led them to her little woven structure.

They did not have to duck to enter, as Pan had to. Once inside, they were amazed at how spacious it was. Pink and purple blossomed from green vines that snaked in and out of the woven structure. A soft bed of moss provided comfort underfoot. It was warm, cozy, and comforting.

"I wish our mates could see this. It is so charming," Tarron said.

"They would want us to make some for them, no doubt," Thord laughed.

"It will be far easier to make one here than back home," Clah observed.

As the weeks passed, Nootau became more and

more comfortable with his place among the others and also at Lulnomia. When he was not engaged with Wrollonan'Tor's training, he found a role answering questions about the Akassa, the Sassen, and life back home.

CHAPTER 7

Back at the High Rocks, Adia waited for life to feel normal again. She had almost immediately been filled with some shame about pleading with Pan not to leave An'Kru or Nootau alone. She had allowed her last-minute fears to get the better of her. But it was done, and it did comfort her, so she tried to turn her focus back to the life at hand.

She helped Iella with the Healer duties but mostly spent time with Aponi and Nelairi. She could tell they missed An'Kru and Nootau terribly. Oh'Dar also spent more time with them, including them in playtime with his own offspring. Everyone did their best to help ease the loss felt by the twins.

A while after the others had left for Lulnomia, Oh'Dar and Acise took their sons, Ashova and Tson-akwa, and Adia's twins on a hike. Oh'Dar was in front, followed by the twins and then his sons. Acise brought up the rear where she could keep an eye on all the children.

It was a beautiful summer day. The humidity was low, making it comfortable to be outside. Oh'Dar had taken them many times to one of his favorite spots, the shallows he used to frequent as a child, with his father, Acaraho. Oh'Dar used to sit on the bank and dip his feet in the water, letting the minnows nibble on them. He had at one time convinced his brother Nootau to try it, and Nootau had later shown Iella. Oh'Dar still smiled at the memory.

But this was a different location. He had not brought the youngsters here before, as it was further away, but he thought somewhere new might be fun.

As they were about to make their way down a fairly steep incline, Oh'Dar turned to remind them to watch their step and use the adjoining branches or rocks for support. It was not dangerous in itself, but carelessness could turn a common event into a tragedy.

As he turned back, his oldest son, Tsonakwa, whose hearing was far better than everyone else's, shouted out, "I hear something."

Just then, a shower of rocks started tumbling down the hillside above, right toward Acise, who was a way behind the rest. Frozen in fear, Acise stood there as the massive load came roaring down, spewing dust and smaller rocks ahead of it.

"Acise!" Oh'Dar screamed. The children were between him and his mate. He would never make it in time.

"Momma!" Tsonakwa cried out. He instinctively ran to his mother, grabbed her by the arm, and used all his strength to pull her off balance. They both fell but were now out of the way of the tumbling rocks. Seeing they were safe, Oh'Dar shouted, "Move forward! Quick! Follow me!"

He ushered them down the path quickly but safely. Once they were a considerable distance away, he said, "That is far enough. We can rest here a moment. Is everyone alright?" He wanted to ensure the children were fine before checking on his life-walker. He was shaking but did his best to hide it.

Aponi put an arm around his sister and said, "We are both fine."

Then Oh'Dar made his way past them, stopping on the way to check with his youngest son, Ashova. Then he reached Acise and Tsonakwa. He looked directly at his son and then at his life-walker. "Are you hurt? Either of you?"

Both shook their heads.

"That was very brave of you, son," he said, his voice shaking in spite of himself

"No one was hurt, thanks to Tsonakwa's quick thinking," said Acise. "Let us keep going!"

A little further, and they were at the shallows. It was a peaceful setting, with just the right mix of shade and sunlight. Small ripples broke the surface of the water.

"Sit down now, and put your feet in the water."

"Uh-uh!" Aponi objected, laughing. "What if it is cold? I will watch this time."

"Oh, come on!" Acise encouraged him.

Aponi threw her a suspicious look. "You go first," he said to his sister.

Nelairi shot him a squinty look and stuck her tongue out at her brother.

Then she scooted closer to the water and slowly eased in one foot. Startled, three nearby frogs jumped into the water. "Oh!" Nelairi exclaimed and pulled her foot out.

Oh'Dar laughed. "This is just like the one we usually go to; there is nothing to be afraid of!"

"Alright," Ashova conceded. "I will go first this time." He let one foot dangle in the water, but a moment later, he pulled it out, screaming!

"Oh no! What happened!" Oh'Dar jumped to his feet and ran over to his youngest son.

"Nothing, I was just joking." Ashova giggled and covered his mouth, his eyes dancing with childish delight.

Their two sons could not have been more different. Tsonakwa, the oldest, was serious and reserved, while Ashova was a jokester, always laughing and smiling. So they should not have been surprised by his antics.

Nelairi swatted at Ashova, "That was not funny!" But she was laughing.

"Oh, alright. Let me try this again," and Ashova put both feet in this time. After a few moments, he said, "Just like at our usual place, little fish are nibbling at my feet and toes. It tickles. It feels good!"

"Alright, I will try it again." Nelairi went second. "It feels—cute!"

Acise laughed. "It does feel cute!"

The trauma of the prior event was passing. As Oh'Dar watched the children having fun, he was calculating their path back since the original way they had come was now blocked.

"I'Layah should have come with us!" Ashoba said.

"She is with Miss Vivian today," Acise answered. Oh'Dar had surmised that somehow I'Layah realized her grandmother was up in years and would not be around forever. He was sad she had to bear such an adult burden so early.

While the children were busy, Acise came and sat down next to Oh'Dar. "Miss Vivian seems sad lately. I think it was the news about Mrs. Thomas."

Oh'Dar had hated to tell Ben and Miss Vivian, but the last time Ned returned to Wilde Edge to visit his family, he learned that Mrs. Thomas had passed. Her sons had sold Shadow Ridge, and they and their families moved away. Oh'Dar had second thoughts about telling them and now sometimes wished he had not. "She is still thinking about that?"

"She mentioned it the other day. That is why I think it is on her mind," Acise explained.

"Maybe I should not have told them. I am not sure they really needed to know," Oh'Dar said.

"That was a hard call, my love. I do not know what I would want in their situation—to know or not to know."

"Grandmother is showing I'Layah her journals and the record she has kept of the People's history," Oh'Dar said. "What Khon'Tor asked her to do long ago. No one expects I'Layah to pick up that task; I will do it. But in time, it may fall to her to carry on."

"Do you want to hear some good news?" Acise asked.

"Definitely!"

Acise leaned over and said in his ear, "Iella is seeded."

"What?! After all this time. Finally! Does Nootau know? Does my mother?"

"Your mother knows; she is the one who told me, with Iella's permission, of course. Nootau does not, but what a blessing for Iella. When he returns, no doubt Nootau will be shocked when he learns he is a father. Whenever that is."

"I wonder how old he or she will be. Still a toddler? A young adolescent?" Oh'Dar mused. "Did she know before he left?"

"Just before Nootau left, she told me she suspected, but it had not been long enough to know for certain. She did not want to get his hopes up with him leaving, so she waited. But now she is certain she is."

The two Mothoc brothers made their way across the distance separating Zuenerth and Kayerm. Morvar'Nul had copied onto a piece of hide what Gard had drawn in the sand, and he pulled it out repeatedly, checking their direction and progress. They were trying to locate the magnetic nodes and follow the patterns of the stars, but sometimes they felt they were traveling blind as spans of time passed with no clue if they were on the right track. Morvar'Nul had practiced what Gard had tried to teach them about quieting his mind and listening for guidance. It seemed to be working to some extent. At least, he felt some inward assurance that they were going in the right direction.

They were hot and dusty and dirty. They knew better than to drink from stagnant water and listened carefully for any sounds of moving water as they traveled. They often found small springs along the way. At each water source, they filled their water pouches before continuing on.

Food was plentiful, and when they did come to lakes or streams, they would spear fish and eat their fill before continuing. They were not on a schedule. So much time had passed since Moart'Tor left that a few more days or weeks wouldn't matter—other than worrying their mother.

"By now, Gard must have told them what we are doing," Nofire'Nul commented.

"I hope he is still alive," Morvar'Nul joked. Only it wasn't truly a joke. They both knew there was a possibility that their father might have killed Gard for helping them. They hoped Gard had been able to explain that they would have gone with or without his help.

"I guess we will find out when we get back."

Eitel had done as she intended. She was in possession of the names of the males Bidzel and Yuma'qia said would be a good match for her. She had recognized their names but did not know anything about either of them, really. She thought of asking her brother if he knew anything but feared he might inadvertently blurt out that they were a potential match for his sister. No, she preferred to be able to conduct her research in anonymity. So she spent weeks watching them, learning about them. She had subtly tried to overhear their conversations with their parents, siblings, and friends.

One morning, she announced to her mother, father, and brother that she was ready to be paired and had made a choice. Her mother, Hola, clapped her hands in joy, and Arpan, her father, waited stoically to hear who this male was that she had chosen.

Before she revealed the name, she explained the painstaking process she had gone through to make her choice. Her father pursed his lips and remarked, "You have done well, daughter. I am glad you have not rushed into it."

Eitel's mother turned and stared at her mate. "Rushed into it? After all these years of coaxing and begging her to agree to be paired? Are you joking?"

"You know what I mean, Eitel," Arpan said.

"Yes, Father, I do. So, I only hope he will accept me."

"He would be a fool not to; even I, as your brother, can see that," said Naahb, always her staunchest supporter and protector.

Eitel sighed deeply. "All right. So the male I have chosen is Paldar of the House of 'Krah."

"Ooh! He is a fine choice. They seem to be a strong line," Hola exclaimed.

Even her father approved, and he was as protective of his daughter as Naahb was of her.

"I know his mother," Hola continued. "She is a kind female. And his father is honorable and a good provider. No doubt he will prove to be a thoughtful and dependable mate."

"What should I do now?" Eitel asked.

"Do as every maiden before you has done," her father advised, "Strike up a conversation with him. See if he responds to you. If he acts interested, does he want to get to know you? Does he ask you questions or just babble on about himself? Ideally, you want a true companion, not just someone to seed your offling."

She had heard this speech many times but never really paid attention, having no desire to pair. But it was all different now, so they sat and talked into the twilight hours.

Finally, Eitel said, "Thank you for all that. I am ready. I am going to try to strike up an acquaintance with him tonight."

The evening fire was customary, no matter the weather. The sparks drifting upward, and the flames licking the air delighted the offling and created a cozy, comforting atmosphere. Eitel waited until Paldar was alone before approaching him.

Paldar'Krah was swatting an ember out of his coat when Eitel approached. "Oh, here, let me help you," she offered and gave a little extra pat to the area of his arm he was focusing on.

He looked surprised but said, "Thank you."

"I am sorry. I did not mean to be so forward. It is a fault of mine, apparently."

"It did not bother me. I appreciate the help."

In her awkwardness, she gave the same area another pat for good measure. "There. Cannot have you going up in flames."

"No, that would probably traumatize the offling," he smiled down at her.

She briefly put her hand over her eyes, "I am Eitel." When she pulled her hand away, he was still looking at her.

"I know. I know your brother."

Naahb did not tell me that! "Then why have I not seen you together?" She realized her eyes were squinted in a question and tried to relax them.

"Are you alright? Do you have something in your eye?" he asked.

Eitel was mortified. "Can we start over?"

He chuckled, "Why? I think we are doing fine. It is not often the most lovely female in the community decides to keep me from bursting into flames."

She felt her cheeks burning. "That kind of you to say."

"I know your brother from hunting parties. We do not have a friendship, so to speak, just an acquaintance. He is a fine fellow. Everyone likes and respects him. We were glad when he paired. Everyone should be lucky enough to have the blessing of a mate and family."

She was lost about what to say next, but he continued, "The spring berries are out. Would you like to join me tomorrow to collect some? I can carry your basket."

Eitel was certainly capable of carrying her own berry basket, but she took it in the spirit given.

"That would be nice."

"Very well; I will leave you to the rest of your evening and meet you here at first light?"

Eitel nodded, "Yes."

He gave a little bow of acknowledgment and then excused himself. She watched him walk away but turned in a circle when she felt eyes on her. Both her family and his, sitting on opposite sides of the fire, had apparently been watching them the whole time.

When she reached her family, Naahb scooted over to make room for her next to his mate.

"That went well!" Hola, reaching out to take Eitel's hand.

"Maybe from where you all were sitting, but I sounded like an idiot," she groaned.

"I am sure you did not sound like an idiot," Naahb reassured her. "If you saw how he responded to you, I would say he is yours if you want him."

"Naahb!" Eitel exclaimed.

"A male knows."

"His mother and father were also watching the whole time," Hola added. "By the looks on their faces when you approached him, they were very pleased. They knew what was going on."

"Let us be honest," her father said. "Everyone here knows what just happened. After all the years in which you turned away virtually every attempt by any male to exchange more than a few words with you, for you to approach him and strike up a conversation made it very apparent."

"Especially when you boldly patted down his arm," Naahb teased. "And then did it again."

"Pleeeease. I am dying inside."

"It could not have gone better, little sister. When a beautiful female approaches you and then she seems flustered by *your* presence, there is not a higher compliment."

"I am going to bed. Or better yet, I will crawl under a boulder somewhere." Eitel excused herself and slipped into Kayerm as quickly and quietly as she could.

CHAPTER 8

At the Far High Hills, Harak'Sar, his son Brondin'Sar, High Protector Dreth, and Khon'Tor were meeting with the Overseer, Urilla Wuti, to plan the upcoming High Council meeting. When the Brothers had been brought into community with the Akassa and Sassen, the focus of the gatherings shifted to matters that affected them all. However, there was still a need for the People and their Leaders to come together separately. This was not only for the Leaders to hone in on their specific issues and needs but also to perform the Ashwea Awhidi, the pairing ceremony, which allowed for a time of celebration and socializing. This time there would also be visitors from all the communities coming to demonstrate and share their discoveries and innovations.

Khon'Tor had heard Nimida would be coming to show off her toolmaking improvements. He had not returned to Kthama since confessing to the People his crime against Adia. Despite the Overseer's impassioned plea not to talk about his attack, as well as the pleas of Nimida and Nootau, Khon'Tor and Tehya had prepared themselves for some eventual backlash. If talk about them had spread beyond the High Rocks, it was done discreetly, and in all the years since, no word of it had come back to them. Their main concern was for their offspring, that their daughter and son would never have to bear shame over their father's mistakes.

Brondin'Sar had come a long way since Khon'Tor first started mentoring him. Harak'Sar had stated his intention to handing over the leadership of the Far High Hills in the next year or so, and Brondin'Sar had waited to be paired, knowing that once he was Leader, he could select his own First Choice. So, for now, he was content to continue to follow the direction of his father and Khon'Tor.

As the meeting broke up, Urilla Wuti asked Khon'Tor to stay behind for a moment.

"You heard that Nimida is coming," she stated.

"Yes. I do not know what to expect."

"Since your confession, during my visits to Kthama, Adia has said that Nimida has found her place in the family. She has become close to the twins, and she has fully embraced her role as big sister."

"Thank you for letting me know."

"She would probably welcome your approaching her; that is what I am trying to tell you. Pan has returned and taken An'Kru and Nootau away, and no doubt Nimida will be grieving the loss of two of her brothers."

"I will try to find something—comforting—to say to her, given the opportunity."

"*Make the opportunity*, Khon'Tor."

"Ah, thank you. I understand."

Before long, the Far High Hills was bustling with activity. Those who would be displaying their wares had arrived early to set up their displays. Khon'Tor and Brondin'Sar walked up and down the rows, examining the latest baskets, carved gourds, spearheads, woven blankets, and such. Up ahead, across the room, Khon'Tor spotted Nimida's mate, Tar, helping someone spread out a particularly large bison hide, so he excused himself and took the opportunity to approach his daughter while she was alone.

"Nimida," he said.

She looked up from setting out her knives and spear heads. "Khon'Tor," she said. "I was hoping I would see you."

Khon'Tor breathed a sigh of relief. "Your mother

and Acaraho should be here shortly if you wish to have company."

"Tar is here with me as well. It has been so long since you left Kthama. How are you and Tehya?" she lowered her voice. "Please tell me no harm has recently come to you from what happened—what took place—back home?"

Khon'Tor shook his head. "To whatever extent, the plea for understanding that you and your brother made seems to have worked. The only problem we had was the attack in the tunnels of the High Rocks. There has been no other trouble in the years since then. Not even a dirty look—at least not that Tehya or I have caught."

"I am so relieved to hear that. I pray enough time has passed now that this can be behind all of us. I understand why you never came back to Kthama, especially since they never caught your attacker. But I am glad to see you.

"Father."

The term hit Khon'Tor right in the heart. He felt tears stinging his eyes and had to turn away. When he turned back, he saw something in his daughter's expression he had thought he would never see. Affection.

"If it is possible, though I know I am only here for a few days, I would like to spend some time with you and your family. Maybe, get to know you. As a person?"

"I would welcome that very much, and so would Tehya." He looked down at her display. "What have you brought?"

"More of my handiwork. Tar and I continually improve our tool-making. Look here, take this." Nimida handed him a blade.

Khon'Tor took it, and was about to wrap his hand around the handle. Instead, he froze. "What is this?"

"That is my new design. Well, not new. Perfected. I have been working on it for the past six years—since your last visit to the High Rocks. Do you remember the knife I gave you then?"

"Yes. I still have it. Even though you did not know who I was to you when you gave it to me, I cherish it. It is stored in a special place." He was still staring at the blade in his hand.

"Well, that was the other design. Feel how the handle now fits your hand even better? It is perfectly balanced, so when you throw it, it flies straight and true. And I have now designed the handles to fit the shape of the user's hand even more closely and added some texture, so they are even less likely to slip."

Khon'Tor's mind was spinning.

"I had made another, different one but somehow misplaced its twin, so I had to start over. But it worked out, as you can see." She was impervious to his inner turmoil.

"It is exquisite—if that is the word for it."

Khon'Tor handed her the blade. "I will speak with Tehya about us getting together. Thank you —daughter."

Nimida smiled, and Khon'Tor took his leave.

He started walking, his mind awhirl. He did not know or care where he was going. A thousand thoughts were vying for attention. It could not be, yet it had to be. He finally sought out the Overseer and took her aside.

"Let me know when Acaraho arrives, please. I need to speak with both of you together. Adia can join us. It is urgent."

The Far High Hills was filling up. It took longer than Khon'Tor had hoped for Acaraho and Adia to arrive, but it gave him time to calm down and think more clearly. Finally, the Overseer sent for him. She had Adia and Acaraho in her quarters with her, as Khon'Tor had asked.

"Thank you. I realize this is perhaps bad timing, but trust me, it is important."

"We understand, Khon'Tor," Acaraho said.

"What can we do for you?" Urilla Wuti asked.

"After the attack on me at Kthama, Acaraho, you sent the hood and blade here to Urilla Wuti with your First Guard, correct?"

"Yes. It has been stored away very securely all this

time and never disturbed."

"I need your help," he said.

Khon'Tor waited for his moment. It finally came. The one person he was looking for was standing off to the side with no one else around him. "May I speak with you?" he asked.

"Of course."

"Walk with me," Khon'Tor said, and the two headed off down one of the branches of the many tunnels of the Far High Hills.

"Where are we going?"

"Just a little bit further; I want to ask you something."

The moment they rounded a corner, Khon'Tor turned and slammed Tar against the rock wall. With one hand, he pinned the young male's arms high against the wall and clamped the other against Tar's mouth.

"Now, shut up and listen, and listen very closely. And quit struggling, or I will make it so you never struggle again."

"You said I made a fatal mistake by burying the hood in a ginseng patch. Well, you made a fatal mistake when you carelessly selected the knife you tried to kill me with. It was not just any knife. It was one of only two of a kind. It was a prototype your mate, my daughter, was working on."

Tar shook his head as best he could, and Khon'Tor removed his hand, so the young male could speak. "You are wrong. It was not me!" he said.

"Stop lying."

"I am not lying. Besides, they said they never found the hood or the blade."

"Acaraho found it. And it was brought here for safekeeping. Nimida has just shown me the mate to that knife. The only person who had access to the other was *you*. Now tell me why. Why did you want to kill me?"

Khon'Tor watched the denial leave Tar's eyes.

"Why? Do you want to know why? So justice would be served. You do not deserve to live. My sister died in that rockfall, saving you and Acaraho. *For what?* So you could go on to become a monster? To rape the Healer Adia? No one held you accountable, not even Acaraho. So I stepped in to avenge Adia and my sister."

Khon'Tor released Tar but stood close enough to catch him if he tried to run. Tar rubbed his wrists where they had been grasped.

"So what happens now. Are you going to turn me in? They will not believe you if you do; it is your word against mine."

"No, it is not," a voice from the shadows spoke, and out stepped Acaraho and the Overseer.

"There is no question that the knife you used belonged to your mate, Nimida," Urilla Wuti said. "She had to make another, which she has just shown Khon'Tor, because the first went missing. That missing knife is the one the Healer Adia removed from Khon'Tor's side and which has been here under safe-keeping since that time. They are an exact match. There is no question of your guilt, not to mention that you have just confessed to it."

Tar scowled at the Overseer. "So what will happen now? Am I to be banished? Killed?"

Khon'Tor answered instead, "The Overseer has agreed that nothing will happen to you—if you accept a few conditions," Khon'Tor said.

"I do not believe you. Why do you not also want *justice*?"

"You use the term justice when your anger and hatred of me suggests it is instead revenge you seek. But regardless, what good is justice if it harms more than it heals? My daughter is happy. What good would it do to bring you to task for this? It will destroy her happiness. No, your punishment will have to be the knowledge that you are not the honorable mate she believes you to be. And the possibility that someday she may well realize it. Pray she never discovers the truth."

Khon'Tor continued, "I have lived with the dark feelings you harbor. The hatred, the lust for revenge. Retribution. I know too well the path you are on. A path that leads only to self-destruction. Not for my sake but for your own and my daughter's, I pray you find your way through this and stop nurturing your anger and resentment. I wasted too much of my life drowning in the muck and mire of where you are now. I finally learned to choose differently."

"So that is it; you are just going to let me go? All of you? Knowing what I tried to do?"

"Well, not entirely," Urilla Wuti said.

"What happens now is up to you," Khon'Tor explained. "If you attempt anything else, if you threaten my mate or any of my family, even my friends, if I even see you staring at one of them, I will kill you myself. And it will not be a swift death."

He turned and looked at Acaraho and Urilla Wuti, then back at Tar, "And no one will ever find your body. Ever."

Tar was now shaking.

"Do you understand the terms of our arrangement?"

Tar managed only to nod his head.

"We are finished," Khon'Tor said. "I leave you to the future of your own making."

CHAPTER 9

Nofire'Nul dropped down onto a grassy knoll that was bathed in moonlight. "We are lost."

"No, we are not," Morvar'Nul said.

"Yes, we are. Where is the map? Give it to me."

"You think you can understand it better than I do?"

"Just give it to me, and yes. I was paying attention."

Morvar'Nul was tired and irritable. "I was paying attention too."

"Not as much as I was; now let me see it!"

So Morvar'Nul pulled the rough drawing out of his traveling satchel and tossed it to his brother, who caught it mid-air, then straightened it out and flipped it around a few times.

"Right, now I see. I think I see where we went wrong."

"What. Let me see!" Morvar'Nul sat down.

"Here. I think we are heading in the wrong direction. I do not remember this magnetic node." Nofire'Nul looked around and then up to the stars overhead. "We are weeks off course."

"Are you sure?"

"Unfortunately, yes."

"'Rok!" Morvar'Nul clasped his hands and rested them on top of his head. Then he lay back on the grass. "I just pray that when we do find Kayerm, it turns out to be worth our while. I pray Moart'Tor is there, or there is at least some clue to tell us what happened to him."

"After all this time away, we cannot go back with nothing. We had better come up with something to justify what we have done," Nofire'Nul agreed.

Morvar'Nul turned onto his side, facing his brother. "We could make it up."

"Make what up?"

"Anything. I mean, if we come up with nothing, who will know?"

"Well, if we say he died, and he does show up one day, everyone will know. If we say we found him and he is fine, no one will settle for that. They will want to know where he is. Perhaps make us take them to him."

"So we will have to be more clever than that."

"We had better find something; that is all I am

saying. Your ideas are usually good, but making things up is not one of your skills."

Paldar'Krah had not stopped thinking about Eitel since the moment she approached him at the evening fire. Well, that was not exactly true. There was not a male at Kht'shWea who had not admired Eitel ever since she reached pairing age. However, they had given up trying to get to know her because she made it clear she was not interested in them. And, if possible, she had become even more distant since the arrival of the Guardian's nephew Moart'Tor. Stories circulated that she was infatuated with him. And if that was what it took to win her interest, then there was no hope for any of them.

So no one was more pleased or surprised when she approached him than Paldar'Krah. He knew his parents and hers had been watching their every move. He was also aware that his mother would want to pounce on him the moment he walked away. He was grateful she had held herself in check so as not to embarrass him, but it didn't take her long to find him after she returned to Kht'shWea. And his father was right with her.

"I know, I know, Mother. I certainly did not expect that, either," he said.

"Just so unexpected. Obviously, it means something," his mother said.

"I certainly hope so," Paldar'Krah chuckled. "I am taking her berry picking in the morning." He thought his mother was going to faint.

"Saraste'," his father said. "Please try to calm down. We are all very happy about this turn of events, and we need to be mindful not to embarrass our son."

"Thank you, Father. I am trying not to embarrass myself either." He laughed again.

The next morning Paldar'Krah was waiting for Eitel as he had said he would. He greeted her and offered to take her basket. She smiled up at him, which made his grin grow even wider.

"I know the best places," she said.

"Lead the way."

"So you said you know my brother, but not really?"

"Well, just when a group of us go out hunting. Of course, we do not really get to know each other; it is mostly about the hunt. He is a skilled hunter; I know that much, and he was recently paired, was he not?"

"Yes, some time ago, though. They have a son."

"Good for them." *Go slow, go slow, go slow.* "So

what else do you like to do besides pick berries?" he asked.

"Oh, goodness. Well, some of my favorite things to do are to walk through the meadows when the spring flowers have bloomed and, in the evenings at twilight, I enjoy watching the firebugs. And if it is clear enough, to lie out under the stars and watch the patterns pass overhead."

"I also enjoy all those things. We are blessed to live in such a beautiful world," he added.

"I can cook," she blurted out.

He smiled, "Well, that is good." He noticed she looked away and wondered if she was embarrassed. "No, really. That is great. Because I love to eat." This made her laugh, and he felt good about that.

They reached the berry patch, and he moved the branches around so she could get deeper in to reach the berries the birds had not yet found.

"Thank you," she said each time he made a new path for her. Soon her basket was overflowing, and he was sad knowing their outing was probably nearly over.

They walked back in silence. When they reached home, she said, "Thank you for helping me today."

"I would be happy to help you any time, Eitel. Day or night. Just ask me. I enjoyed your company this morning."

They parted but only after they had made plans to meet by the evening fire.

"Oh, Mother," Eitel wailed. "I need some advice. I so enjoyed my time with him today."

There was no need to explain who *him* was; everyone knew.

"I do not want to rush this and ruin it. And I want to make sure I like him, that I would be happy living with him, and that he would be a good father to our offling."

"Your father has done some checking around."

"Oh no." Eitel covered her face with her hands.

"No, it is fine, truly." She pried her daughter's hands away. "Look at me. Your father was very subtle. He just talked to some of the other fathers to see what they thought of Paldar'Krah. For what it is worth, all of them spoke very highly of him. And his whole family."

Eitel let out a soft groan. "It is alright; I know you are both excited, and Father is just trying to help, and you are right; everyone knows what is going on. I have to accept that and get to know him as best I can."

That evening, Eitel looked for Paldar'Krah, trying to be discreet about it. Finally, she saw him and her heart skipped a beat. He saw her and smiled, and made his way over to her. She motioned at the place next to her, and he sat.

Paldar'Krah was hiding something behind his back. "What do you have?"

"Just something silly. Promise you will not laugh."

She narrowed her eyes. "Hmmm. No promises."

He held out his closed hand.

She stared down at it and looked up again. "I do not see anything," she teased.

He turned his hand over and slowly opened his fingers.

"Oh!" It was a beautiful, rounded red jasper stone. "I have never seen one as pretty as that."

"I have not, either. I thought you might like to have it."

Eitel took the stone and, with one of her fingers, rolled it around in her palm. "Thank you. I do like it so much."

"They are all watching us. Would you like to take a walk?" Paldar'Krah asked.

"Sure."

He led her down one of the short paths that was especially pleasant for walking. They came to a clearing by a knoll, and he pointed upward. "Beautiful stars tonight. Would you like to stay a while and enjoy them?"

He knelt and reached up to help her down next to him. She took his hand and tried to land as gracefully as possible.

"I hope I am not being too forward," he said.

"No, it is fine. It is a lovely idea. We can lie here and enjoy the stars and talk. After all, it is one of our favorite things to do."

They talked for hours. Eitel was afraid he might try to kiss her, and then she was afraid he would not. In the end, they just talked and made plans to go spearfishing in a day or so. She hid her disappointment that she would not see him tomorrow but reminded herself of her own comments to her mother about not wanting to rush things.

Morvar'Nul and his brother backtracked and found the magnetic node they had missed. They had been gone way too long and could not turn back now. They finally came upon the Brothers, just as Moart'Tor had. And, like him, they cloaked themselves and watched for some time.

"Are those the Akassa?" Nofire'Nul asked.

"No. Those are the Others. Those we were supposed to protect, those who Moc'Tor betrayed."

"They are so small. Hairless. Fragile. However in the world did they mate—"

"It is a mystery. I am not sure anyone knows any longer how it was done," Morvar'Nul said.

"Do you want to stay longer?"

"I want to study them. If they are as similar as Gard says, maybe when we finally find the Akassa,

having learned about the Others will help us understand them better, see where their weaknesses are."

Over the coming weeks, Eitel and Paldar'Krah
became close. He still had not kissed her, which was
starting to bother her, though she chalked it up to his
just being patient and not wanting to assume too
much. Then one night, it finally happened.

"Another beautiful night of stars. Care to take
another walk?" he asked.

"I would love that," she replied, and they
wandered off to what had become their special spot.

As usual, he gave her his hand to help her down.
As she sat next to him, he leaned in, and the next
thing she knew, his lips were on hers. Whisper-soft
but telling of fires of passion set and waiting to be lit.

It surprised her, and she drew back.

"Oh, I am sorry. I have misread something."

Eitel reached up and placed her hand around the
back of his neck, drawing him down to her again.
She kissed him this time.

"I have been waiting a long time for that," she
said. Then she kissed him again. This time he kissed
her back—hard. He leaned back and drew her down
onto him. His kiss and being in his arms were everything she had hoped they would be. After a few
moments, they were forced to come up for air.

"This past while has been the happiest of my life," he stated.

"Mine too, but I have a confession to make. I hope you do not hate me for it."

"I could not. Please tell me."

"It was not a chance meeting when I came up to you at the fire that first night."

"I did not think it was, considering that you have never been known to approach any male, ever," he smiled.

"I mean, there is more to it than just that. It is no secret that I avoided any attachment to a male. Not even giving anything a chance to develop. Then, I met the Mothoc, Moart'Tor. And something in me awakened. I know it was just an infatuation, but it started me thinking about what I was missing in life. Then my brother paired. And then I finally decided I was perhaps ready."

"Perhaps?"

"Well, no, yes. I was ready. Am ready. Oh, bother."

He took her hand, "It is fine. Please, just relax; it is me."

"So, I went to Bidzel and Yuma'qia and asked them to find a match for me. They gave me the names of several males I could safely pair with."

"Was mine just first on the list then?" he asked.

"No. Not at all. There were quite a few. I watched each of you for some time. And in the end, you were the one I chose. I mean picked. To get to know, that is," she stammered

"And are you going to keep going down the list now? Is that what you are telling me?"

"Gracious, how could you think that? No! I am not going to go down the list. I have no need to. I have found what I want."

At that, he took her in his arms and kissed her again. "So have I."

A bit later, he asked her, "But what of your feelings, your infatuation with Moart'Tor? Is that really behind you?"

"Yes. I promise you it is. I just need to do one thing; I have one last homage to pay to close that door forever. Do you understand?"

"I do. I understand the need to mark important events, milestones, turning points—whatever—in our lives. That is why I gave you the red jasper. To mark the moment in time when I realized you were the one I wanted."

"I will cherish it all my life."

"And I will cherish you. I will do my best to be the mate you deserve."

He drew her into his arms and pressed her hard up against himself, and whispered into her ear, "I will anxiously await the moment when I will make you mine. Once I do have you alone, it will be a while, though, before I get to the heart of the matter.

But I can assure you, you will be ready for me, *every time,* before I take you."

Paldar'Krah's words took her breath away. She had never wanted a male before, never truly understood what all the fuss was about, and yet now she was burning with desire for him.

There would be many sleepless nights until they were paired.

Though it came as no surprise when Eitel and Paldar'Krah announced they were to be paired, it was still a cause for celebration. The mothers were excited over the prospect of offling. The fathers were happy their mates and offling were happy. The females of pairing age were happy that Eitel was finally no longer available, and the males of pairing age were glad they could quit thinking something might change to give them a chance.

Haan and Haaka were also happy for them. They had both worried when Eitel refused to make any movement toward pairing. Naahb had even consulted Haan about her preoccupation with Moart'Tor, though had his sister known, she would have been furious.

The pairing ceremony was mere days away. Sastak, Haan's unofficial representative of the females, had helped Eitel pick out the living quarters she preferred, and her friends were busy helping her prepare and decorate them.

There was only one last thing she wanted to do, and time was running out. She was grateful that when she told Paldar'Krah about it, he did not think it was silly or a waste of time. He accepted that it was important to her and that it did not mean anything was lacking in their relationship.

So early the next morning, Eitel set out alone for Kayerm.

CHAPTER 10

Having had their fill of studying the Others, the two brothers continued on their way. They found the remains of the old oak tree, the same one Moart'Tor had found. According to Gard's map, they had only to cross the meadow that stretched out in front of them, and they would find Kayerm.

"My heart is pounding," Nofire'Nul told his brother.

"From excitement or from fear?" Morvar'Nul asked.

"Right now, from excitement. But if we go over that crest and see thousands of Mothoc, it is going to be from fear."

"It is nearly dark. Why not wait and see how many fires are lit. That may give us an idea of their numbers. We have waited all this time; another night will not hurt."

The two slowly crossed the meadow, almost afraid to breathe for fear the other Mothoc would hear them. As they cleared the crest, crawling on their bellies, they stopped.

Total stillness.

Not one fire was burning. Nofire'Nul looked at his brother and whispered, "What? Why are there no fires?"

"Maybe we are in the wrong place, or it is too early, or perhaps they abandoned the practice? But I cannot even see an entrance."

The brothers kept watching. There was no movement anywhere. It was not late enough for everyone to have bedded down, and they were bewildered.

"We will wait here till morning. It is riskier as we might be discovered, but we need to know how many we are facing."

"And if we are even in the right place," Nofire'Nul answered.

They did not sleep well, expecting to be discovered and captured at any moment. Finally, the first light broke, and the two turned their attention back to Kayerm.

Morvar'Nul pointed out a barely noticeable, vine-covered opening. "Keep your eye on the entrance."

"I did not see that last night."

They waited. And waited.

Nothing.

"Rok!" Morvar'Nul swore. "What the krell is going on!"

The two waited some more. Finally, convinced Kayerm was abandoned, they approached the cave system.

As their brother, Moart'Tor, had done, they entered and explored the interior, going down the various tunnels and into the living spaces. They met back at the entrance.

"There are signs it was inhabited not that long ago. But where would they have gone?"

"Could Moart'Tor have found Kayerm, as we just did, only he killed them all?"

"Unlikely. There would be signs of struggle, broken trees, shattered boulders. This place looks like it was tidied up before whoever it was left."

"Now what? No Mothoc, no Sassen, no Moart'-Tor. And no clues," Nofire'Nul lamented.

Morvar'Nul grabbed his brother's arm. Hard. "Shhh; someone is outside."

Eitel stood in front of Kayerm's entrance, where she had first met Moart'Tor and tried befriending him. Where he had withdrawn from her touch, intended as a gesture of comfort. Then later, that one day when she and her brother had invited him to partake of their bountiful catch. She walked over to the place where the nightly community fire had burned. She could picture Moart'Tor sitting on one of the boulders, the flames casting an amber glow over the silver-white in his coat. She then sat down there, going over her memories and trying to figure out why she had become so enamored with him.

Suddenly, she felt she was not alone. She turned around and gasped. Behind her stood two huge Mothoc males.

"Where is my sister this morning?" Naahb asked his mother. "I thought we might do some early morning fishing together."

"She had something she needed to do, something to help her finally let go of the past—and let go of Moart'Tor."

"What would that be?"

"She went to Kayerm, I think to revisit some of her memories, to put them to rest, so to speak."

"How long has she been gone?"

"She left at first light. I expect she will not be long."

"What do we have here?" Morvar'Nul said.

The Sassen female looked terrified, her eyes wide

and her mouth slightly open. As she started to get up, Nofire'Nul stepped around her and grabbed her by the arms, pulling them behind her back.

"Who are you?" the female asked, wincing. Morvar'Nul could make out what she said; it was not exactly their language but very close. She twisted her head around as if looking for others.

"I am Morvar'Nul, and this is my brother Nofire'Nul."

"Morvar'Nul? Are you— Did you come looking for Moart'Tor?" she asked.

At the mention of their brother's name, Nofire'Nul babbled, "She knows Moart'Tor. He has been here!" Then he leaned down and said into her ear, "Where is he? You had better tell us; we will find out anyway."

"Let me go, please. You are hurting me."

Morvar'Nul nodded to his brother, who released her. She shook her shoulders as if trying to shake Nofire'Nul's touch.

"Tell us where our brother is," he demanded.

"He is not here. He left."

"Where did he go? And where is everyone else? Did he leave with them?"

"We do not know where he went. Only that we were told he left with the Guardian Pan."

The two brothers looked at each other. Morvar'Nul stepped closer to her. She tried to back

away but ended up pressed against Nofire'Nul's chest.
She stopped abruptly.

Morvar'Nul saw his brother's eyes start to glaze
over as he began rubbing his hands up and down the
female's arms and pulled her more tightly against his
body.

"Wait, let me go." She twisted her head around to
try to glare at him.

"Where are your people? You did not answer
me," Morvar'Nul scowled.

"I am not going to tell you anything. I do not know
why you are here, but you must be from the rebel camp
the Guardian talked about. Please leave us alone."

"What should we do with her?" Nofire'Nul asked.
He leaned down and sniffed her neck, and she tried
to pull away. "She smells good." Then he moved a
hand around to cup her breast. He moved his thumb
over her nipple.

"Stop it!" she cried out, trying to shrug out from
under his touch.

"Not now, brother. Now is not the time for any of
that," Morvar'Nul admonished him.

Nofire'Nul pulled his hand away and looked
disappointed.

Then Morvar'Nul's attention was drawn to
another figure approaching. It was another Sassen.
"Who are you? Let her go!" It was a male, and he
headed in a dead run toward them.

Nofire'Nul pushed the female Sassen behind him, and Moart'Tor moved to stand next to him, blocking access to her.

"This is none of your business. I suggest you turn around and go back to wherever you came from," Morvar'Nul said.

The male kept coming.

"Naahb," the female called out. "They are from the rebel camp! Go back and get help. Please!"

Morvar'Nul raised his arm and slapped the female across the face, knocking her to the ground.

The Sassen male yelled, "Eitel! Are you alright?" A moment later, he was upon them, and with one blow, Morvar'Nul also felled him to the ground. The male landed on his side, unmoving, his arms splayed out in front of him.

"Noooooo," the female cried. "What have you done!"

"Listen to me!" Morvar'Nul reached down and seized her by one arm, yanking her to her feet. Then he grabbed her face, pinching her cheeks together. "I doubt my brother killed him, but if he means anything to you, I suggest you shut up and come with us quietly."

She stared down at the motionless body, which now had a trail of blood seeping out from beneath it. Morvar'Nul followed her gaze and bent down next to the fallen stranger. "He is alive. But he will not be for long if you refuse to come with us." He picked up a boulder, and the implication was clear.

"Alright. Alright. Just please do not hurt him further," she pleaded.

"We had better go," Nofire'Nul said, looking around quickly. "Are we really just going to leave him?"

"What harm can it do? It is bad enough that we take one of their females. If we kill a male, it might incite the Guardian's ire. She apparently cares for these creatures."

"So you do fear the Guardian?" Nofire'Nul seemed astonished.

"I do not know what powers the Guardian has. I just do not see the wisdom in provoking her. But I agree, it is time to go. Whatever this female knows, she can tell us on the way."

"No, please. Please do not take me away. I am about to be paired," she pleaded. Her hand was cradling her swollen cheek.

"Your life means nothing to us," snarled Morvar'Nul. "You and your kind should never have been created. But you are lucky; you do perhaps have a purpose, so do not be afraid; we do not intend to kill you. But we will if we have to."

"It is nearly darkfall," Hola said. "They should have been home by now."

"They probably wandered upstream, perhaps even ate some of their catch," Arpan answered.

"No. Something is wrong. Very wrong."

"If it will ease your mind, I will go and look for them. I know their favorite fishing places."

"Yes, Naahb said he was going to look for her there. But Eitel said she was going to Kayerm first thing this morning."

"Why would she go to Kayerm?"

"Something to do with finally letting go of her past feelings for Moart'Tor."

Arpan traveled up and down the banks of the Great River, doing as he had said he would. He found no trace of his son. And there were no signs that he had even been there or that anyone else had, for that matter. None of the grasses that grew on the banks were disturbed. No space had been flattened by someone walking through or sitting down. As far as he could tell, neither Eitel nor Naahb had been there. He went on to Kayerm.

Twilight was falling, but it was no barrier as the Sassen could see well in the dark, which it was by the time Arpan reached Kayerm. He stood on the ridge and scanned the area, not expecting to see his offling there but perplexed about where else they could be. As his gaze passed over the ground in front of the entrance, he saw a shape. A dark shape. Lying motionless on the ground.

Arpan ran as fast as he could and knelt down before the figure. It was Naahb. He rolled his son over on his back, praying he was still alive. Naahb rolled his head to one side and moaned. Arpan said a silent prayer of thanks, then quickly looked around for his daughter. Seeing no sign, he tried to rouse Naahb further. All Naahb did was moan and pass out again.

What should he do? Should he leave his son there and fetch help? No, it was too far; Naahb would be left alone for too long. Hating to move him, Arpan felt he had no choice. He somehow managed to lift his son's heavy, limp body and, as gently as he could, started the long trek back to Kht'shWea.

Everyone was sitting around the community fires. "Look!" someone shouted, seeing Arpan carrying something that looked like a body.

"Where is Artadel?" another shouted. Males ran to help as Arpan gently laid Naahb on the ground, ready for Artadel to examine him.

Hola was beside herself, "How badly is he hurt? Please tell me he is going to be alright—"

Pelted with questions, Arpan explained how he had found his son but no sign of his daughter. "There were footprints in the area. I can only assume they were Naahb's and Eitel's. But there were others too, and from the size of them, they could only be Mothoc."

"Mothoc! You do not think Moart'Tor did this?" Eitel's mother exclaimed.

"No. Nor the Guardian. Not for a moment. But the prints were clearly too large to be Sassen. Maybe they were from the rebel group Moart'Tor was raised in."

"Perhaps they came here looking for Moart'Tor. But why hurt Naahb? And what happened to Eitel." Hola was frantic.

"Please calm yourself," Haan said. "Please. The Healer will do everything he can to see that your son makes a good recovery. When Naahb awakens, we will find out what he witnessed and who did this to him. And if he saw any signs of his sister."

"I do not know where Eitel is," Arpan said slowly. "But from the prints, I believe I can tell you what happened to her. Whoever *they* were, they took her."

"We will send out search parties," Haan decided.

Eitel was sick to her stomach. She could not get her thoughts off her brother. The image of him lying on the ground, not moving, was more than she could bear, and she paid no attention to their surroundings and where they were going. She was stunned into silence, her mind awhirl with prayers for her brother's safety. She wondered if anyone had found him yet. Was he safe now? There were very few predators they had to fear, but an unconscious Sassen had no defense. A bear could easily take advantage of Naahb's helplessness.

Oh, please let him be alright. Please, Great Spirit. Eitel could weather anything that was coming her way if only her brother lived.

When they had left, they moved at a furious pace, and she had trouble keeping up. Now that they had covered some distance, the two Mothoc must have decided they were safely away because they slowed down. Eitel was strong, but they had longer legs and more stamina, and better physical reserves than she did. She finally asked if they could take a rest.

"We are far enough away," the largest one said. "Besides, they do not know where Zuenerth is— unless Moart'Tor told them. But still, I doubt they could find it based on his information alone."

The two giants sat down with Eitel sandwiched between them.

"Guardian knows," the smaller male said.

"Stop with this talk about the Guardian, brother. If you were that afraid of her, you should have said so before we started out on this—quest. Whatever it is. It is too late to worry about her now."

Eitel listened to the conversation. The largest one seemed to be in charge, and she wondered if he was the oldest. The smaller one, who she thought of as the younger, the one who had molested her the first chance he got—he was the one she was worried about. The older one seemed to have a bigger purpose in mind than letting his brother have his way with her.

She felt the younger one's eyes moving up and down her body. She pulled her knees together closer. He caught her glance, and a sickening smile crossed his lips.

"I do not like how your brother looks at me." She took a chance that the oldest brother could control the younger one.

"Stop it, Nofire'Nul. Just get it out of your mind!"

"Why? It is a long trip. No one will know. We deserve a reward for what we are doing, but there is no guarantee Father will see it that way. So why not enjoy her while we can? You can have her next."

"No. We are not going to spoil her. Father will decide who gets her. Hopefully, it will be one of us."

"Well, if he gives her to me, I will share her with you. I would hope you would do the same," the one named Nofire'Nul said.

The older one sighed, then agreed. "That is fair. I agree we deserve something for risking our lives looking for Moart'Tor."

"Risking your lives?" Eitel could not help it. Nor the laugh that followed her words. "Abducting a female much smaller than you and beating up a male also smaller than you. How is that risking your lives? And what honor is there in that?"

"Va!" swore the one named Nofire'Nul. "Remind you of anyone?"

The older one smiled. "She has fire in her like Mother. Perhaps Father will want her for himself since they are now living apart."

"I doubt Mother will agree to that," the younger one laughed.

"Time to get some rest. We will start out before first light."

Now Eitel could have kicked herself for being in such a stupor that she had no idea where they were or how they had gotten there. Even if she could get away while they slept, she did not know how to get back home.

The large one pointed out two places to lie down. "I will take the first watch and wake you later, brother."

Eitel's hopes faded further. They would not be careless enough to sleep at the same time. She was hungry, but since there was no mention of eating, she lay down and willed herself to fall asleep.

In the dark, she awoke to someone pressed up behind her. Eitel froze, her eyes wide. She tried to slide forward, but a strong arm came around from behind and grabbed her tightly around the waist.

"Shhh," a male voice said.

Eitel knew it was the younger one, Nofire'Nul. He

was defying his brother's orders. The hand around her waist moved lower and slid down to cup her between her legs.

"Stop it, or I will scream and wake your brother!" she whispered.

"Go ahead. He cannot watch me every moment. There will be another time; only then I will not be as kind and gentle as I am now." His fingers started moving, probing her.

"Stop it. You have no right." She struggled against his arms.

"Does that feel good?" he asked as he started to move his fingers in a circular motion. "I am told that females like this."

She had no choice, so she pulled her attention away from what he was doing. Maybe she could not stop him, but she could try to blot it out of her mind as much as possible.

He pulled his hand away, rolled her over onto her stomach, and moved around behind her. Then he knelt and used both hands to pull her by her hips up onto her knees. Eitel could tell he was fumbling around with himself back there, and then she felt his manhood pressing up against her. She thought of Paldar'Krah and that their pairing was only a short while away. She blocked out the tears that threatened to fall.

Suddenly, the other brother let out a loud moan and sat up, rubbing his hand over his face. Nofire'Nul immediately released Eitel and scooted away as quietly as he could. Before the older male looked over at them, her assailant had just enough time to stand up and act like he was coming back into the camp.

"What is the matter?" Nofire'Nul asked his brother.

"Bad dream, that is all. Why are you standing up?"

"Just relieving myself. You can go back to sleep; it is still my watch."

"No, it is fine. I would rather stay up. I do not want to take the chance of entering that dream again."

Eitel wanted to ask what the dream was about. Perhaps it was a warning. Perhaps if he told her what it was, she could use it to discourage him from following through with her abduction.

"What was your dream?" she asked, trying to sound normal, her heart still pounding for fear of what Nofire'Nul had been about to do to her.

"It was daylight, and clouds started forming everywhere," Morvar'Nul said. "Huge angry-looking clouds, the undersides nearly black. Like nothing I have ever seen before. It became quiet all around. Unnaturally quiet. It seemed all the birds and animals had taken cover as if they knew something terrible was about to happen."

He stopped talking a moment as if trying to shake

it off. "Then the winds came with leaves and twigs and branches caught up in it. It was blowing so hard I could not stand up against it; the force knocked me to the ground and held me there. Then it became as dark as night. The sound was deafening. Not just the sound of the branches and other things pelting down but also the roar of a terrible wind. And then the ground shifted as if something inside Etera herself was moving. Then I woke up."

"Where were you?" Nofire'Nul asked.

"Home. You were there, and Father. But I did not see Mother. I had a feeling she was gone."

"Gone? As in, she left us?"

"No. Worse. Gone, as in dead."

Nofire'Nul snarled, "Do not say that. Do not ever say that!"

"It was just a dream; calm down, it does not mean anything. No, go to sleep. It will not be first light anytime soon. Rest while you can because I certainly cannot."

Nofire'Nul stomped off in his anger.

Eitel heard Morvar'Nul say it was just a dream, but he seemed far too shaken up for that to be true. Taking a chance, she said, "It sounds like more than a dream. It sounds like a warning."

"And what do you know?" he snarled, glaring at her. "I suggest you shut up and stop irritating me, or next time I will let my brother finish what he started with you."

"You saw?" she was aghast. "And you did not stop him? What about your great speech about not spoiling me."

"I saw. I watched for a while—and enjoyed it. Do not worry; I would have stopped him before he penetrated you."

"So you lied about the dream," she challenged him.

"No, the dream was real. I had already woken up and was lying there trying to shake it off. Then I saw what my brother was doing and decided to let it go for a while."

Eitel lay down and turned her back to him. She had let him see her upset, and she vowed she would not do that again. She tried to drift off, knowing Nofire'Nul could not bother her much while it was his brother's turn to look out. She thought about her brother and Paldar'Krah. What was going on back home? Had they found Naahb and was he alive? And what were they thinking had happened to her? Were they looking for her?

Paldar'Krah was beside himself with worry and anger. He felt helpless that he did not know who had attacked Naahb or where his beloved was. None of the searches turned up anything useful. Whatever tracks there were faded a short distance from Kayerm.

Naahb had still not awoken, but the Healer said he thought he would eventually. The wounds had been treated, and it was now just a matter of time, but until Naahb came to, there could only be conjecture about what had happened.

"We have to go after her," Paldar'Krah told Haan yet again, pacing in front of the Adik'Tar. His father and High Protector Qirrik were also there.

"Of course," Haan said. "But where to? I agree that it was most likely Mothoc from the rebel camp, but with no tracks, we do not know where their community is. We cannot just set out for nowhere. When Naahb wakes up, hopefully, he will know for sure what did happen."

Haaka could hold her tongue no longer, "Haan, I know our males are strong and powerful, but we must also be reasonable. If she is being taken to Zuenerth, you cannot just take a few males and go after her. No one knows what it is really like there, how prepared they might be for you to show up. Perhaps that is the plan, to lure you there? We can only guess they found Kayerm the way Moart'Tor did. And as far as we know, the only two people who could find Zuenerth are Moart'Tor and Pan."

Haan thought for a moment. "It could be true. Their true goal might have been to find Moart'Tor. And by taking one of our people, a female especially, they could well surmise that would cause us to come to them. It is possible they found out from Eitel that he had been here."

Just then, Artadel came into the room and said Naahb was awake. "Please do not exhaust him; he is weak. Keep your questions to a few."

They found Naahb barely sitting up enough to take a sip of water from a gourd his mother was holding for him. "Son, how do you feel?"

"Like I could sleep forever. Father, did anyone find Eitel?"

"No, not yet. Can you tell us what happened?"

"As I was coming up to Kayerm, I saw two males, huge like the Guardian. One of them was holding her; I saw her struggling. She shouted for me to leave —that they were from the rebel camp and I should get help, but I could not leave her. Then one of the males slapped her hard across the face. I saw her fall to the ground. I ran toward them, and the one that had hit her also struck me down as if it were nothing. That is all I remember."

"Thank you," Haan said. "Rest now, Naahb, and get well; we will do all we can to rescue your sister."

He gathered the others and said, "It was indeed the rebel Mothoc. We need Moart'Tor or the Guardian to take us to the rebel camp. I will speak with Acaraho. He deserves to know what has happened, and his mate may well have a way of contacting Pan."

CHAPTER 11

"**Y**ou asked for me?" Pan said to Wrollonan'Tor.

"Yes. Something has happened at Kayerm. Eitel has been abducted, and her brother attacked."

"By whom?"

"Two of Moart'Tor's brothers, from Zuenerth."

"Is her brother alive? And has she been harmed?"

"Yes to both. He will recover. They sent out search parties but did not find Eitel. When her brother recovered enough to talk to them, he told them the two were from the rebel camp."

"I cannot leave. I promised Adia that I would never leave An'Kru here alone," Pan lamented. "I should send Moart'Tor to Zuenerth?"

"No. You must send Moart'Tor to Kht'shWea. Haan is planning on going after her, but they do not know Zuenerth's location. Moart'Tor must stop them from setting out, or they could be wandering forever. He will explain that he will go and bring back Eitel."

"Alone? Why do some of us not just go to Zuenerth and rescue her?"

"We cannot descend on them, Pan. We cannot risk further division, and we cannot afford to shed Mothoc blood. It will only widen the divide, and the rebels will never find their way out of the darkness. This is Moart'Tor's path to walk. He has believed all along that he can reach them, and he must be given this chance."

Pan did not question Wrollonan'Tor any further. She had learned long ago that despite what he claimed about her becoming the greatest Mothoc that ever walked Etera, he had wisdom and abilities still surpassing hers.

Acaraho and his Circle of Counsel waited until Haan, with Qirrik, his High Protector, and Paldar'Krah were done explaining.

"This involves both our peoples, Haan," Acaraho said. "Not only yours and ours here at the High Rocks but also all the Akassa everywhere. This is a dangerous situation for everyone who becomes involved. We do not know their abilities. Even though there were no tracks found around the High Rocks or Kht'shWea, we cannot assume they think their kind no longer lives among us. And if there is to be an attack by the Mothoc, we must prepare ourselves as best we can. I am going to send for the Overseer, and Apricoria, because she has the gift of seeing the future. We need their counsel."

"But we are going after her, yes?" Paldar'Krah asked, his voice urgent.

"Of course," Haan said. "We are all anxious to get started, but we do not know where the rebel camp is nor what whoever we send might be walking into. We need more information, and Adik'Tar Acaraho is trying to get that for us."

"What about the Guardian? Could she not come and help us?" Paldar'Krah asked.

Haan hesitated, "There might be—complications there. A promise the Healer extracted from the Guardian never to leave her offling alone at Lulnomia and which I suspect the Guardian cannot break."

The messenger reached the Overseer. She immediately called together Harak'Sar, Brondin'Sar, Apricoria, and Khon'Tor.

"They are requesting our help," Urilla Wuti said. "Apricoria and I will go to the High Rocks as they ask."

"Can you see anything of what lies ahead?" Harak'Sar asked Apricoria.

"The Order of Functions only provides the path with the most beneficial outcomes possible."

"What do you see; please tell us," Brondin'Sar asked.

"What is to be, must be, if the rebels are ever to return to the Mothoc fold. What lies ahead is the only opportunity to turn them from their ways, but it will require many to put their own lives at risk. I cannot see the outcome, however. Perhaps because free will is always a factor."

"You will carry this message to Acaraho and Haan?" Harak'Sar asked.

"No," she answered. "I am to remain here. Khon'Tor will carry the message."

"As you say," Khon'Tor answered. "I am sure you have a reason for me to go. But none of us know where this rebel camp is."

"The rebels are on the brink of descending on Kthama," Apricoria said, her voice flat as if listening to something elsewhere. "They believe they will be able to force Eitel to tell them where Kthama is. Our people will not survive a Mothoc attack."

"And the Guardian Pan would let this happen?" Urilla Wuti asked.

She and Harak'Sar exchanged worried glances. Urilla Wuti opened her mouth to say something, but Apricoria rose and interjected, "What I see is only a shadow of what might be. The future is fluid, ever in flux. And it is always the Great Spirit's will that none shall perish."

Khon'Tor left the room to prepare to leave for Kthama. Apricoria followed him and stopped him with one last message. "Say your goodbyes to your family before you leave."

Naha was nursing Akoth'Tor when she and Moart'Tor heard the announcement stone clack at their door. Moart'Tor rose to answer it.

"Pan. Please come in. Have you come to visit Naha and our son?"

"I am always happy to see Naha and little Akoth'-Tor. They grow so quickly," Pan said, admiring the newling.

"I have some news I thought you would want to know," she continued. "Two of your brothers, Moart'-Tor, set out from Zuenerth to find you."

"My father sent them?"

"I do not know. Only that they did find Kayerm."

"I can only imagine their surprise when they found no one there."

"There was someone there. Eitel."

"Oh, no," Naha exclaimed. Moart'Tor looked as if someone had just slapped him.

"Your brothers found her. Her brother, Naahb,

tried to intervene, but one of them hurt him badly. He has been unconscious for some time. They took Eitel. I promised the Healer Adia that I would not leave An'Kru and Nootau during the time they are away from her, so I cannot possibly help. It falls to you to do this."

"Because no one else knows where Zuenerth is, you need me to rescue her?"

"Yes. The Adik'Tar Haan and some others are planning to go but do not know where the rebel camp is. They could wander forever. I need to send you there first to stop them. Then I will send you directly to Zuenerth," Pan explained.

Moart'Tor turned to his mate, who quickly said, "Do not let any concern for your son or me trouble you; we will be here when you return. Only, please, be safe."

Acaraho and Haan had assembled a meeting of as many and as few as they felt absolutely needed to be involved. From Kht'shWea were Haan, his mate Haaka, their High Protector Qirrik, and Eitel's promised mate, Paldar'Krah. From the High Rocks were Acaraho, Adia, Iella, the High Protector Awan, and First Guard Thetis.

Urilla Wuti had come to the High Rocks without Apricoria but with Khon'Tor. Adia was surprised to see him as he had not been to Kthama since the attack years ago.

Khon'Tor delivered Apricoria's message to them. Just as he finished speaking, a shimmer appeared in the center of the room, and there stood a huge Mothoc. Startled, Adia jumped to her feet.

Acaraho quickly stood up and placed himself between his mate and the behemoth standing before them. It was only the second Mothoc any of them had ever seen. He was as large as Pan and, although he had some silver markings, was certainly not a Guardian.

"I am Moart'Tor. I mean you no harm."

From behind her mate, Adia could see enough of Moart'Tor to know he was staring at Acaraho.

"You are Akassa?" he asked the Leader.

Haan interrupted, "Moart'Tor. Why are you here?"

Moart'Tor looked at Haan. "The Guardian vowed to the mother of the Promised One that she would not leave him without her at Lulnomia, so she cannot help. I have been sent to rescue Eitel, who I believe my brothers from Zuenerth have taken."

Adia cringed inwardly, once more feeling guilty for extracting that promise from Pan. Yet, in her heart, she could still not withdraw it. Yes, the Guardian had asserted that every Mothoc at Lulnomia was true to the Great Spirit, but what if there was one, just one, who harbored resentment against the Akassa and Sassen? And would Pan not want the Promised One to live to fulfill his destiny?

"You are Akassa?" he turned to Acaraho and asked again.

"Yes, we are Akassa," Acaraho waved his hand to include Adia and the others. "I am Acaraho'Tor, the Leader of this community. This is my mate, the Healer Adia." Acaraho turned just enough so that Moart'Tor could see her.

"You are 'Tor," Moart'Tor said to Acaraho. Then he looked at her and said, "And you are the mother of the Promised One?"

Adia came out from behind her mate. "I am."

"You are honored among females. Just as I have pledged my life in service to Pan, I do the same to you and your son, the Promised One."

Adia calmed herself down enough to take in Moart'Tor's essence. She believed him; he meant them no harm.

Adia wanted to ask how Nootau and An'Kru were doing and was sure Iella had questions too, but this was not the time. Out of the corner of her eye, she could see Paldar'Krah studying the Mothoc. He also must have much to ask Moart'Tor.

"Do you know why your brothers would have taken Eitel?" Haan asked.

"I do not know, but the Guardian Pan sent me to stop you from trying to find the rebel camp. I will go and rescue Eitel."

"But how are you to rescue her?" asked Paldar'Krah. "I imagine they will not want to release her; otherwise, why would they have taken her?"

"I go not only to bring her home to you but to convince my people that you, the Akassa, and the Sassen, are not abominations and that they should drop their vendetta."

"How do you think to do that?" Haan could not help but ask.

"It was only when I came to Kayerm and saw you as people, the same as the Mothoc, that I realized my father was wrong. Perhaps I can convince them to abandon their hatred. It is also my fault that, presumably, they came looking for me and found Eitel instead. It is my duty to return her safely home."

"I am going with you," Paldar'Krah spoke up, stepping forward to stand directly in front of Moart'Tor.

The Mothoc looked down at him, and everyone waited for one of them to say something.

"It is not for me to say who goes and who does not," Moart'Tor said. "Only that I cannot guarantee the outcome. It is my urgent prayer that I can reach the people of Zuenerth, at least to save Eitel and convince enough of them to reject my father's plans."

Khon'Tor spoke up, looking at Acaraho. "I will go to represent the Akassa."

"Khon'Tor—" Acaraho started to say, then turned to look at his mate, who had stepped forward.

Adia moved over to Khon'Tor and said, "You do not have to keep putting yourself at risk to prove your loyalty to the People. Your service as Adik'Tar speaks for itself."

"I object," Paldar'Krah spoke up. "The Akassa will only slow us down. Eitel could be in danger at this very moment."

Moart'Tor answered, "I know my father. He will not move so quickly to dispose of her. He will consider how he can leverage having her."

Haan then added, "Paldar'Krah, we all are concerned for Eitel's welfare, and we will do all we can to ensure her safe return. But Moart'Tor is trying to make us understand there is more at stake here, as hard as that is to say. He needs to show the people of Zuenerth that the Akassa are not the abominations they have been led to believe. An Akassa must be there."

Khon'Tor reflected, "I now understand why I was sent here by Apricoria. She said they are preparing to attack us, and I believe Moart'Tor is right; the only way the rebels' minds might be changed is if they see us as flesh and blood—people like themselves."

First Guard of the High Rocks, Thetis, now stepped forward. "I must speak. Hear me. I do not usually speak of fear, yet it is my responsibility to protect our Leader and the rest of you as well. I fear this is foolhardy. I fear it is a suicide mission. Even with Moart'Tor's presence, you will no doubt be greatly outpowered." As he spoke, his eyes traveled up and down the giant filling the room. "Pan would have the most influence over them, but I understand why she could not come. However, in her absence, why did other Mothoc not come with you? Surely, together, you could overpower them!"

"You must understand," replied Moart'Tor. "A battle must be avoided at all costs. Etera cannot lose even one more drop of Mothoc blood. The only hope is for their minds to be changed, and it falls to me to do it. We must remember it is always the will of the Great Spirit that none should perish."

"We must trust the Order of Functions," Urilla Wuti said. "Even if Eitel is safe and being treated well, we cannot abandon her. And, as seems to be the case, it is, perhaps, the last chance for the rebels to turn from their dark path."

"But what of our people?" Iella spoke up. "What of their lives? What of Tehya and your offspring, Khon'Tor? How does she feel about this?"

"Tehya understands my duty to protect the People. She always has."

Adia saw Haaka shifting in her seat. She knew Haaka and Eitel had become close friends and imagined Haaka was reluctant to add to the conversation as she wanted Eitel rescued but was conflicted because the plan sounded very dangerous. Adia was very relieved it was not Acaraho who planned to go, but she was now worried about Tehya.

"There is little to debate," Paldar'Krah said. "We cannot abandon Eitel, just as we could not abandon any of our people. We must go, and if our odds are better having this fellow with us, then I withdraw my objection." He nodded in Moart'Tor's direction.

"Haaka is due to deliver any time—" Haan said.

Acaraho interrupted. "No one expects you to go; you cannot at this time."

Iella spoke up, "I will send a hawk to follow you. At least that way, we will know what is going on. You can speak to it, and we—I—will hear you."

"Do those of you that are coming need some time to prepare before leaving?" Moart'Tor asked.

"I need to gather a few things," Khon'Tor said.

"Yes," Paldar'Krah agreed. "Not just stores for the trip but also weapons."

"Do you have Pan's power, for lack of understanding how it works, to take everyone there immediately?" Haan asked.

"I do not. While I am a Mothoc like Pan, I am not a Guardian. Also, from what Pan explained, there is not enough of the Aezaitera in the blood of the Akassa to safely transport them. If the Akassa is to go with us, and I now believe it is critical that he goes, we will have to travel on foot."

Paldar'Krah looked crestfallen. Everyone anticipated that it could be a long journey. And despite

Moart'Tor's assurances for her relative well-being, what about Eitel during that time?

As long as it had taken to get to Kayerm, it was taking longer to get home. The female could not walk as fast as they could.

Morvar'Nul kept an eye on his brother to make sure he did not accost her again. Not that he cared about her feelings, only that he did not want to return home with a ruined, sickly, and weak female. He was counting on her quelling Kaisak's anger at their leaving.

In order to keep her from running away, Morvar'Nul had started tying her up at night and sleeping right next to her. It also meant she could nudge him if his brother tried to interfere. One night they were lying there, and he could hear her quietly crying.

"No harm has come to you, female; stop crying," he admonished her.

"Why have you taken me from everyone I love? What can one female Sassen be worth to you?" she asked.

"In and of yourself, you are worth nothing. But you will have your usefulness; at least, I hope so."

"Why, what are you going to do with me?" she asked.

"My father is Kaisak, Adik'Tar of Zuenerth. Perhaps my brother spoke of him and of us?"

"Moart'Tor spoke of him, yes, and of his brothers. And your mother."

"Hmmm. We thought perhaps he had died on the way, but it is good to learn that was not the case. But he never returned home, and you say you do not know where he went."

"No one knows where he went, only that Haan, our Adik'Tar, said he left with the Guardian."

"The male who tried to save you, he called you Eitel?"

"Yes, that is my name. He was my brother. He is my brother."

"I struck him hard; I doubt he survived," Morvar'Nul said. He could feel silent sobs wracking her body. "The life you knew is over. It does not matter if he is alive or not. You will not see him again. You will live among us. You will serve us."

The sobs started to quiet down. "You seek to make me a slave? Is that your plan, no longer to kill us all but to enslave us?" It seemed hard for her to get the words out.

"We will see. You are the first to be captured. It will depend on whether you survive."

"Survive what?" the female asked.

"Bearing a Mothoc offling."

Eitel could not believe what she was hearing. *They intend to use us for breeding? But what of the males? Will they kill all our males and use us as breeding stock?* She remembered her family saying she had to forget about Moart'Tor, that it would have been too dangerous to be seeded by a Mothoc, and yet this was what they were planning? Even if she somehow survived, how many of her fellow Sassen females would not and would die an agonizing death trying to birth a Mothoc offling?

Eitel prayed hard that her brother was alive, that this fate awaiting her could be avoided. Praying that somehow the rebel's eyes would be opened as Moart'Tor's had been.

Moart'Tor waited while Khon'Tor and Paldar'Krah prepared to set out. They had packed what they could carry to help them on the journey. Fishing spears, blades, gourds and water baskets, dried nuts, and meats. There were only two other things Khon'Tor needed before they would be ready to go.

He sought out the High Protector Awan. "I need something from you. Something you have been keeping for me for some time?"

From the corner of his living quarters, Awan pulled out a long bundle wrapped in a heavy skin. He undid the hide and carefully handed what was inside to Khon'Tor. How long ago it had been when Khon'Tor first asked Awan to make such a formidable weapon. It was formed from a single piece of seasoned locust, and rows of razor-sharp obsidian points were embedded all along the shaft. A long, equally deadly obsidian spearhead was lodged in the end.

As he had when he first saw it, he remarked on the weapon's perfect balance.

"A formidable weapon, to be sure," Awan remarked.

"I never used it for what I intended at the time."

Khon'Tor stepped into the largest part of the room and swung the weapon around. Once again, like so many years before, it sliced through the air as cleanly as it would through any opponent. But a Mothoc? "I hope I will not need to find out if it is sufficient for what I now have in mind."

As he approached Nimida in the Great Hall, Khon'Tor saw Tar's eyes meet his.

"I apologize for interrupting," he said to his daughter.

She looked up upon hearing Khon'Tor's voice. "I

did not know you were here," she said, putting down the piece of fruit she was about to stuff into her mouth. She briefly glanced at the hide carrier slung over his shoulder.

"I am only here for a short while. I thought you might be able to help me out." From the corner of his eye, Khon'Tor could see Tar still staring at him. "Hello, Tar," he said, glancing at him briefly.

He turned back to Nimida. "I need one of your best spears. Several of us are going on a mission to rescue one of Haan's people. It will be for one of Haan's males, so the heftier, the better."

"I have just what you need, but it is too much for me to carry," she said.

Tar spoke up, "I will go get it for you. I know the one you speak of." Khon'Tor watched him leave, then said to Nimida, "It is good to see you again. Are you well?"

Nimida smiled, "I am going to tell Adia today, but how wonderful that you showed up so I could tell you too. I am seeded!"

"I am happy for you both." A smile broke Khon'-Tor's usually stern demeanor. "You will make a wonderful mother."

"Who are you going to rescue?" she asked.

"She is one of Haan's people. She was abducted by some who we believe came to look for Moart'Tor."

"Oh, no! How could that be? Did they come here

looking for him after all this time?" Her voice was low, so others could not overhear.

"I hope to get answers to all of those questions and more."

Tar returned carrying a large, heavy spear.

Khon'Tor took it from him, but it was so heavy that he almost dropped it. Once he had it under control, he said to Nimida, "You were right. This is perfect. I will compensate you when I return." He started to walk away and then turned back, "I will ask Acaraho to make it right with you should I not come back."

Nimida frowned, "Khon'Tor?" she said. Her voice cracked just a little, "Please make sure you do come back."

He nodded and walked away without looking at Tar.

CHAPTER 12

"How much longer is it?" Eitel asked. She was tired, filthy, and hungry. She stayed close to the older one as much as possible, avoiding the younger one. Although Morvar'Nul had put a stop to the advances, she still did not trust what Nofire'Nul might do if his brother were out of sight.

The emotional strain was also wearing on her. Naahb was never far from her mind, and she constantly prayed he had survived Morvar'Nul's attack. She knew he, her parents, and Paldar'Krah would be distraught. She wondered if they would come looking for her—if they even knew what had happened. She thought about the footprints from their struggle left in the ground outside Kayerm. Even if Naahb had not made it, surely they had recognized that those were not Sassen footprints? And if these Mothoc were planning on using her for breeding, did that then mean they would go back for other Sassen females another time?

"Can we please stop; I am so tired," she begged.

The younger male said, "She does not look good, brother."

Morvar'Nul stepped over and looked her up and down. "We will rest for a while. But we are almost there. I want to make it by nightfall, if possible."

Eitel did not know what would be worse—finally arriving at the rebel camp, anticipating Nofire'Nul's advances, or more sleepless nights tethered to Morvar'Nul. Sometimes in the night, if Morvar'Nul was deeply asleep, Nofire'Nul would sneak over close enough to her to whisper, "I am going to have you. I do not know how yet, but I will find a way."

It was Drall who first saw the figures coming. He shielded his eyes from the morning sun and squinted. They were too far off to truly tell, but it could not be anyone else. It had to be Kaisak's sons, but who or what did they have with them?

He waited a while longer before turning and hurrying back to the camp to tell the Adik'Tar that his sons were returning.

"What?" Visha exclaimed. Then she started hurrying until she got close enough to make out the figures. "It has to be them. Who else could it be? Oh, thank the Great Spirit, they are alive."

"That is not Moart'Tor with them," Kaisak said, also squinting. "It looks like—" He turned to Gard, "That must be a Sassen with them."

The news swept the village. The younger members had never seen a Sassen. They clumped together, madly discussing the possibilities and that they might now learn what had happened to Moart'Tor.

Iria and Dak'Tor showed up. By the time the three travelers had reached Zuenerth, the entire population was assembled and waiting.

Visha darted out and ran to her sons. She placed her hands on each of them, touching their faces and their arms and exclaiming how glad she was to see them. She only briefly glanced at who they had with them, recognizing it as a female Sassen. The question she wanted to ask most was burning in her mind. What about Moart'Tor?

But then Kaisak walked out to greet them, followed by a number of the others.

"Gard told us where you went, and I did not expect to see you again," the Leader said. "What do we have here?" He turned his attention to the Sassen female.

"A gift," Morvar'Nul said.

Visha stared at her son.

"For our people," he quickly added. "We talked of

this, how we might use the Sassen to keep the Mothoc blood flowing on Etera. So that Etera might live."

Visha watched as Kaisak stepped forward and took the female by the chin, raising her head to look at him. He turned her head from side to side, noting that she bore virtually the same dark coat as Iria, one highly favored by the males. Then he released her and walked around her, looking her up and down. Visha glanced at the growing circles of males crowding in around them.

"Kaisak," she growled. They were still estranged, and it was one of the few words she had spoken to him in a long time.

Kaisak looked up and also noticed the crush of males. "No one touches this female. I must consider what will be the best use of her. Gard, find a place to keep her. I will hold you responsible for her welfare."

Iria, who had been tending to Useaves, pushed through to the front and stepped between Kaisak and the female. "Look at her. She is thin and dirty." She turned to Kaisak's sons, "Did you even feed her? How could you treat another person like this?" She glared at both of them and turned to Kaisak.

"I did not realize you were so fond of the Sassen," he quipped, leaning in toward Iria. Iria wanted so much to comfort this female, to tell her that not everyone there was against her, but she realized she could not. All these centuries of silence, of appearing to side with Kaisak, and she could not let him know any differently now.

"Fondness has nothing to do with it," she said. "If you wish her to bear offling, then she must be healthy. It is as simple as that." She kept her eyes from meeting the female's lest she betray her true concern for the Sassen's welfare. "Let me take her to the river and let her clean up. It will take all day for her to dry; we may as well get a start on it," she said.

Kaisak said, "Gard, go with them. The rest of you disperse. Now!"

"You are sending Gard with us? What do you think, that she is going to run off?" Iria scowled. "Where would she go? She is smarter than that." Iria wanted a chance to show this female some compassion, and she could not risk it with anyone else around.

"Wait!" Visha yelled out, grabbing Iria's arm so she could not leave. She turned to Kaisak. "What about Moart'Tor? Are we not even going to ask about my son?"

"The answer is not going to change, Visha," Kaisak argued. "I have as many questions as you do. But they are all exhausted from the trip, and there will be plenty of time for questions later."

"No. I want to know now. Morvar'Nul," Visha

demanded of her son, "what did you learn about Moart'Tor? Where did you find *her*? Tell me what happened?"

"We made it to Kayerm," he replied. "We waited before approaching to see how many were living there and who they were. There was no one. We went inside, and it was obvious no one had lived there for years. While we were there, she showed up." He pointed to Eitel. "As far as Moart'Tor is concerned, she told us he did find Kayerm but eventually left with the Guardian Pan. She says they do not know where to."

"We decided to bring her back with us," Nofire'Nul added. "It was the perfect opportunity."

"There was no one around? No one? So no one saw you abduct her?" Kaisak asked. "So no one followed you?"

Iria noticed a quick look exchanged between Kaisak's two sons.

"No one followed us. The only ones who know the location of Zuenerth are Moart'Tor and the Guardian."

Kaisak narrowed his eyes, "But if no one saw you, then no one knows what became of her. They would have no reason to suspect us."

Iria knew her mate was listening as closely to this conversation as she was. As were Dazal and the other members of their circle.

"Are we done here?" Iria asked. "I will now take

her and let her get cleaned up. She also needs rest and a hearty meal."

Kaisak seemed to be thinking it over. "Get on with it then."

So Iria sent her daughter, Lurir, to fetch some soapwort from her quarters, and then she led the Sassen down to the river.

"What is your name?" Iria asked.

"It is Eitel."

"My name is Iria. My mate is Dak'Tor, brother of the Guardian Pan."

"We have met the Guardian," Eitel said, "but she did not speak of him. This is the rebel camp of Zuenerth?"

"Yes," Iria said. "This is Zuenerth."

"You spoke back to that one, the Leader —Kaisak?"

"Yes. He hates my backtalk, and I do not do it very often, but he has to put up with it because I am the Healer. The best you can do now is to try to win Kaisak's favor. Challenging him is not going to help your situation; it will only let him see you as even less of a person than he already does." Iria handed her the soapwort.

"Ugh," Eitel said as she waded into the water.

"I know; it will take a long time for you to dry. But in the end, you will feel better. I wanted to have a moment alone with you to say that I will do what I can to help. Excuse my forwardness, but did either of his sons touch you?" Iria had to ask.

"The younger one, Nofire'Nul, tried. But the older one stopped him. From then on, Morvar'Nul made sure there was little chance for him to try it again."

Iria waited as Eitel made a lather and spread it over her front and sides. "Here," she said and stepped in to help Eitel with her back.

"What will become of me?" Eitel asked.

"Kaisak wants information about the Sassen and the Akassa. Use that to your advantage. Do not volunteer anything; make him work for it. And do not trust anyone."

"I feel I can trust you."

"You can. But you must not act like it. You must not let on that I feel kindly toward you. I will help you all I can, but if Kaisak finds out, he will hurt us both."

"But you are the Healer," she said.

"I said hurt us, not kill us. And you would think he would not wish to lose my favor, but I am not sure his mind is balanced any longer. There. Rinse now."

Eitel squished as much soap out of her coat as she could, then submerged to rinse it out. After a few dunks, she pushed the water out of her fur with her hands, shook off what she could, and stepped up onto the bank. "I do feel better," she said.

"We will get you settled down, and then I will get

you something to eat. Your coat is dark, like mine," Iria observed.

"I hope that is a good thing."

"It is good and bad. The males, well, they seem to favor it. So that is the bad part."

"It seems I am to be used for breeding," Eitel said, crestfallen.

"That is what they talked about doing. Have you —do you—have offling somewhere?"

"No. I was about to be paired. I had gone to Kayerm to settle some things in my mind. If I had not gone, I would still be safe at home with my family and my beloved."

Iria heard someone approach. "Shhh." She turned and walked up the embankment to see Visha coming.

"Gard has a place ready for her," Visha called out.

"Her name is Eitel," Iria offered, hoping perhaps that naming her would make Eitel less of an object.

"Come, Eitel. I will take you to where you will be staying. I am Visha, the Adik'Tar's mate; it was my sons who found you. I have many questions to ask."

Iria saw Eitel look back at her as if unsure how she was going to avoid answering those questions.

Kaisak was thinking. The fact that his sons had returned was good news, but that they had brought a female Sassen with them was perhaps not. Why had the female been at Kayerm all alone? And if there were no signs of habitation, why had his sons not tried to find out where she was living? He knew Kthama was not that far from Kayerm. Surely they could have made a better attempt to learn more before hurrying back. Something about Morvar'Nul and Nofire'Nul's story did not add up.

So Kaisak was impatient to interrogate the female to learn more about the Sassen for himself.

He had seen how the males looked at her, practically licking their lips. She was comely, and he would not have expected to find her so. She had what he assumed would be a luxurious dark coat when she was cleaned up, much like Iria's. If he did not decide fairly quickly what to do with her, he would have trouble on his hands. Possibly lots of it.

"Kaisak," a voice spoke. It was Useaves. She was sitting against a tree trunk, no doubt propped up there by Iria to give her a break from lying down. Unless she had been sleeping, she would have seen everything.

"Your sons are lying to you."

"Why do you say that?" he snapped at her.

"Because I pay attention when others speak. If your mind was not so filled with the endless clamoring of your own voice, you would also have seen it." She turned her head to the side to rest it against the trunk.

"I do not always speak of what I know, but I did see it," the Leader said. "There is something my sons are not telling me. Most probably something I will not like."

"It is just a matter of time before they come looking for her. Your sons have brought the fight here to you instead of you taking it to them on your terms and in your own time. You had best learn everything possible from her while you can. Because they *will* come for her."

"I am not worried about it," Kaisak lied.

"I have heard of your plans to use her for breeding. You are a fool if you let any of the males touch her." The old Healer coughed, her body doubled over.

Hearing Useaves' convulsions, Iria came over and stooped down. "Would you like to return to your quarters?" She looked accusingly at Kaisak.

Useaves nodded, and Iria helped her to her feet, bracing her as best she could with an arm around the old female's wasp-like waist. "Ask Gard to bring her some food, please?"

She then walked the old Healer slowly back to her quarters and helped her to the sleeping mat, which had been heavily padded to try to relieve pressure on the old female's bones. It seemed Useaves could not find a comfortable position, no matter what. It was summer, and soon the A'Pozz would bloom. Iria had already used up what was in storage, so she was anxiously waiting for the orange blossoms to unfurl, knowing they provided the only solution for Useaves' pain. The pain was getting so bad, however, that Iria was not sure even the A'Pozz would work.

Useaves settled in with a groan. Iria pulled the heavy pelts up over her.

"Gard will soon be in with something for you to eat, and I will check on you later," she assured her charge.

"I have brought you your favorite," Gard said, lowering himself to sit cross-legged next to his mother.

"I do not wish to eat. I wish only to die. But unfortunately, it appears I must suffer a while longer."

Gard looked at Useaves, who was now nothing but skin and bones. The fire that used to burn in her so brightly was now only a dim ember. He had hated her for a long time. But these days, he felt sorry for her. What did her life amount to? Was there anything she had achieved, any moment she could point to and be proud of? He wondered if, now that her days were numbered, she pondered what she had done with her life.

But he had done better. He had never distinguished himself. His fantasies of being Adik'Tar had died long ago when Kaisak stepped in as Leader. He had never had a mate, had no offling. He was angry at first that Useaves had manipulated it so Kaisak became Adik'Tar and not him. But he had to admit, he was not, nor ever had been, a Leader. He followed whoever was the strongest. First, it was Norcab, then Ridg'Sor, then Laborn. And after Laborn died, Kaisak. Gard still had centuries to live, but to what end? His life was just a series of failures with nothing to show for it.

He pushed the bowl toward her. "Please try."

"What do you care?" she snapped at him, knocking the bowl over and sending the contents flying. "Go away. I hurt, and I wish to be left alone. I pray the Great Spirit takes me, and soon."

"You are my mother. I must take care of you." Only a handful of times in their lives had Gard called her Mother, and then only when they were alone. It merely served to make her angry, though this time not in the same way as before.

"Do not call me that. I bore you, but I was never a mother to you. I will not be around long, Gard. Try to find some purpose for your life. So that when you are lying here in your last days, as I am, you can look back on something—at least one thing—that you did, that you were proud of. One thing that meant something positive for others." It was the first unguarded thing she had ever said to him. The only time she had admitted any regret at all over anything she had done or not done.

"Now leave me." Useaves managed to turn her back to him.

He picked up the bowl and its contents. He would bring her another one in case she might later eat something. He stood up and looked down again at the small, frail figure, barely making a lump under the heavy skins she covered herself with for warmth. Though their relationship had always been difficult, after she died, he would be totally alone in the world.

Eitel curled up on the sleeping mat in the small chamber that was to be her prison. But she was grateful for the softness and the clean wolf skin to cover herself with. She did not need it for warmth, but it was comforting.

Iria had sent some females in with food and water. They did not speak to her much, though their eyes were kind. One of them was remarkably striking, having the grey eyes of a Guardian. Although Eitel was grateful to be left alone, she looked forward to when she might speak with the Healer again and ask her about that female. Realizing her arrival had caused a commotion, she did not know if others would come to visit her or not.

She lay there for a long time until darkfall.

Then, alone in the dark, she let her pent-up emotions come to the surface. Her dreams of her life with Paldar'Krah had evaporated like the morning fog burned off by the rising dawn. The times she had imagined how they would wake in the morning and talk about what they would do that day. Their excitement when she became seeded. Laughter over some shared event that had happened. Him returning from a hunt to show her his bounty, discussing how best to prepare it. How she wished she could tell him where she was. Oh, and what of Naahb. Dear Naahb. *Please let him be alive*.

Whatever life awaited her now would be devoid of all those imagined joys. What lay before her would be a test of her endurance. She had come so close to having her dreams realized, and they had been ripped from her grasp. Instead, she must steel herself for what was to come. She decided to mark off the days she was there.

"They have set out for Zuenerth," Pan said to Wrollonan'Tor. "Moart'Tor, the Akassa Leader Khon'Tor, and Eitel's promised mate, one named Paldar'Krah. The Mothoc will sorely outnumber them. This was not supposed to happen; Moart'Tor was to go to Zuenerth alone. I made a promise, so I cannot intervene. Perhaps— Perhaps you should go?"

"We will trust the Order of Functions."

"In all this time, I cannot believe Kaisak's heart has softened toward the Akassa or the Sassen. Moart'Tor's presence is not going to change his hatred of them. Do they have any hope at all—not just of rescuing Eitel, but of surviving?"

"You are giving in to fear, Pan," Wrollonan'Tor said. "Faith and fear cannot live inside you at the same time. To which will you choose to listen?"

"From everything I have been through, I should answer faith, and yet I cannot. I admit it; I am afraid. Afraid that Moart'Tor is leading them to their deaths. Why would they go with him?"

"You know the answer."

"Because they chose to. Each for his own reasons. Free will. It is the variable in every twist and turn of our paths. Why the Great Spirit gave us such power, I sometimes wonder."

"You know there is no greater gift. That through free will, we have the ability to make of our lives what we want, except that we are often blind to the true power of that gift."

"Does Moart'Tor believe he can open their eyes by taking an Akassa and a Sassen to them?" wondered Pan. "Does he believe he can somehow reach them, open their minds as his were opened? I am sure that is what is behind it. He wishes so much to save all of Zuenerth. I only pray those with him do not pay for his crusade with their lives. Oh, Wrollo-nan'Tor; what if they do?"

"The Order of Functions always produces the most beneficial outcome possible, adjusting in concert with the free will of all involved. Change one element, and the entire picture changes. There is no predicting the outcome. We must wait and see."

"Not all outcomes are beneficial—although I feel disloyal to the Great Spirit for saying such a thing." Pan hung her head.

"The Great Spirit is not offended by your questions. You know that. No, not all outcomes appear to be beneficial, but they are always the most beneficial possible. Sometimes it seems there is not what we would call a good outcome. At least not from what we can see on the surface. But life is rigged in our favor, for suffering has its place in bringing us back into harmony with the Great Spirit."

Pan looked chastened; they'd had this conversation many times.

"My dear Pan. It is often only through struggle that we grow. It is often only in times of suffering that we reach out to the Great Spirit. But it is not the Great Spirit who allows suffering. And the Great Spirit certainly does not cause it. But the suffering that comes as the result of the Great Spirit's gift of free will, whether it be ours or another's, can lead us back onto the path home. When in times of happiness we often forget about The One Who Loves Us the Most, but in times of despair, it is the Great Spirit's face we seek in earnest, and most heartily."

"How powerful we are," Pan reflected. "Not just us, as Guardians, but all of us. We have incredible power to bring goodness into our realm. To help others, to love. Whether it be just a kind word, a small favor, a smile, a pat on the shoulder, or time spent with an offling—all through such simple acts of our free will. Yet, every day, we squander our chances to be bringers of good. It is, in the end, a matter of choice."

Kaisak was sitting at the evening fire outside the family quarters. He wanted so badly to spend time with Eitel that he was practically salivating. He knew she held some of the answers he needed, but she was also beautiful. He had not expected to be attracted to her. She reminded him of Iria, who he had long lusted after. He and Visha were still estranged, living in separate quarters now for some time, but this went beyond that. However, if Visha knew what he was thinking, separated or not, she would certainly eviscerate him in his sleep.

Since Visha suggested it, Kaisak had turned over and over the idea of breeding the Sassen. He knew his mate was right; only if he changed his opinion about the Sassen would the rest of Zuenerth follow. So even though there was no feasible way of getting the Sassen females, he had started slowly working on the minds of his followers. He knew he could not suddenly stop claiming they were an abomination, so he worked on convincing others they could still be useful. "They were never meant to be, so they are ours to do with as we wish. Why should we not use them? They are not like us. They do not matter."

Though he probably should not have been, he was surprised at how quickly the males warmed to the idea. The females as well, though he had expected that. The males' drive was sexual—satisfying an immediate need. The females' motivation was more than that. They wanted offling to love and protect, and mating with a Sassen male presented no health risks to them.

Now that a real live Sassen had been produced, the pressure was on the Leader to make a decision about what to do with her—and quickly.

The truth was, he wanted her for himself. But he knew to do this would be to risk the favor of his people. He knew it would be seen as the selfish decision it was. So his other option was to give her to someone whom he could coerce into letting him mount her too. And that meant one of his sons. And why not? What they had done was an act of valor and deserved a reward. Yes, that would work.

Kaisak knew if there was any way for the Sassen

to escape and find her way home, she would take it. Until she was seeded, that is. He believed that once she was seeded—and certainly once she had an offling in her arms—she would have to make peace with her fate. It would be foolhardy to try to escape and cross the large distance between there and her home without any idea where she was going. It would be another thing altogether to doom her offling to death by such a hopeless attempt.

His reverie was interrupted by the harsh sound of his mate's voice.

"A word with you," Visha said, sharply enough to cut the air they were breathing.

"What is it you want?" he asked, looking up from his seat.

"The female Sassen. What are you going to do with her?"

"Just what Nofire suggested. Use her for breeding. After I find out what I can about what happened to the Mothoc and the Sassen at Kayerm, that is."

"I saw you looking at her. I know you better than you think. You want to keep her for yourself," she accused him.

"No. I was hoping you would return to my bed."

For a moment, he thought he saw her eyes soften, but then they narrowed again. She bared her teeth and hissed, "If you touch her, I will kill you. I will not be humiliated by you taking another female and a Sassen at that."

Useaves had warned Kaisak long ago that Visha was driven by public opinion. Just as it had worked on his behalf when he was courting her, using the prestige of being the Leader's mate to win her, here was the other side of it. If he embarrassed her, that fire he had long ago admired in her would be turned against him in a heartbeat. Eitel's image came to mind, and he wondered if it would not be worth risking it, though, to have that female under him, to be buried inside her, using her as he wished.

His body was starting to respond, so he snapped himself out of his fantasy. "I was thinking she should be given to one of our sons. As a reward."

"And by one of our sons, does that include Moart'Tor?"

Kaisak immediately realized he had done it again. He unwittingly kept leaving Moart'Tor out, a dead giveaway that he did indeed think differently of the offling who had been seeded by Dak'Tor and not himself.

"If he were here, of course." He tried not to stammer.

As she was leaving, Visha said, "I am going to speak to Morvar'Nul and Nofire'Nul and see what they have learned from her on the way here. They had plenty of time to ask her about Kayerm and Kthama."

"What do you think Father will do with her?" Nofire'Nul asked his older brother.

"I hope he gives her to one of us. We earned her."

"Yes, we did, but there are two of us and only one of her," Nofire'Nul said. "You are the oldest, so he is most likely going to give her to you. But you already knew that, which is why you would not let me mount her when I had the chance."

"No. I did not let you mount her because she was already in a fragile state of mind. And she has never been paired. It would have spoiled her. If you are ever going to be a Leader, you must learn to think beyond your own personal desires, brother."

"Well, if he gave her to me, I would share her with you," Nofire'Nul offered.

"I know what you are hinting at. I will think about it. But let us first see if he does give her to one of us. It is hard to tell what he is thinking any longer."

They heard their mother approaching, and they stood up.

"I want to know what she told you about Kayerm. About Moart'Tor."

"She did not tell us anything. She hardly spoke the whole time," Morvar'Nul answered.

"I find that hard to believe."

"Mother, it is true. We would not lie to you," Nofire'Nul defended them both. "She hardly said a word. We counted it as depression. She was withdrawn. We did not want to badger her for fear her health would suffer. We knew you and Father would find out what she knows. We were focused on keeping her alive and—" He stopped. "And getting here as quickly as possible."

"What are you not telling me?" Visha asked.

"We may as well tell her," he said to Morvar'Nul.

He turned back to his mother. "We cannot count on the Sassen keeping quiet about it."

"It was not exactly true that no one saw us there," Morvar'Nul confessed. "A male Sassen saw us. She called out to him and told him to leave. He charged at us in an attempt to rescue her, and I hit him hard. He was unconscious when we left."

"He was still alive?" Visha asked.

"Yes. Though we do not know if he did eventually die."

"So if he lived, then wherever the rest of their people are, they may realize you had to come from here."

Their mother closed her eyes and shook her head. When she opened them, she looked at them each in turn and warned them, "If you are smart, you will go first thing in the morning and tell your father this. Before the Sassen female tells him first."

Dak'Tor and his followers had silently witnessed the arrival of Morvar'Nul, Nofire'Nul, and the Sassen female. When they were finally alone that evening, Iria told them of her conversation with Eitel.

"Kaisak now knows that Kayerm is empty. And it will not take him long to find out from the Sassen female—"

"Eitel," Iria interrupted him.

"Yes, Eitel—that the Mothoc no longer live among the Sassen or the Akassa. This will encourage him to move against them. Especially now that he has decided to use them for breeding."

"But he will most likely still seek to annihilate the Akassa," Iria remarked.

"They serve no purpose for him. They are too small to breed and not strong enough to be any help as workers. Yes, if it comes to a battle, Kaisak will eliminate the Akassa from Etera."

"All we can do now is wait. And pray," Iria said.

CHAPTER 13

Adia could not get Tehya out of her mind, so she left her offspring in the care of Miss Vivian and Nadiwani and went to the Far High Hills. With Nootau gone, Iella wanted to visit her parents, so they went together.

"I am glad to see you both," Tehya said, greeting first Adia and then Iella with warm hugs. "Urilla Wuti, and your parents, Iella, will also be thrilled to see you."

"Did you come alone?" Tehya said, looking around the Far High Hills' Great Entrance.

"Thetis came with us," explained Adia. "I told Acaraho it was not necessary to send the First Guard, but he insisted."

"What about Khon'Tor? Did he not return with you?"

"Tehya, Khon'Tor went with the Mothoc Moart'-Tor, and a Sassen to try to rescue Eitel and to convince the rebels that neither we nor the Sassen are abominations."

Tehya looked up as if gathering herself. "I knew it. In my heart, I knew Khon'Tor's visit was not as simple as delivering a message to your mate."

Iella interjected, "I think you both need some time alone together. I am going to find my parents and my aunt. I will catch up with you later."

Having gained some composure, Tehya suggested, "Would you like to walk, or would you rather sit? My parents are looking after Arismae and Bracht'Tor, so we have time to spend together."

"As to sitting or walking, walking helps clear my mind," Adia answered.

The summer flowers were in full bloom; it was warm but not yet hot enough to be uncomfortable. There was beauty everywhere, but both females were too involved in their thoughts to take it in.

"Now I know why you are here. You came because you are worried about me with Khon'Tor having left to rescue Eitel."

"You would do the same for me," Adia answered.

"So, who went with him? Haan? The Guardian?"

"When Pan took An'Kru and Nootau, in a moment of fear, I made her promise never to leave An'Kru or Nootau alone, so the Guardian couldn't go. She sent Moart'Tor, the Mothoc who visited Kayerm several years ago, and he said he would rescue Eitel. But in the end, Khon'Tor and Eitel's beloved went with him. The Mothoc believes he can find a way to reach his people and turn them from their bad intentions toward us and the Sassen. So Moart'Tor, Khon'Tor, and the Sassen male promised to Eitel left a few days ago. They were heavily armed."

Adia stopped walking and took Tehya's arm. "How are you doing right now?"

"Battling my fear. Fear is a powerful state of mind. It can be all-consuming. Do I wish he had not gone? Yes, of course. But it is who he is. I cannot ask him to be less than he is. Khon'Tor is more than his worst mistake. We all are. He loves the People, and no matter his past crimes, he is and always will be committed to our safety and welfare."

"You are handling it better than I would," Adia said softly, taking Tehya's hand in hers.

"At the moment, perhaps. Tomorrow, or in the blink of an eye, I could feel differently."

"Faith is easy to come by when everything is going smoothly. It is when we are tested that it is most hard-won."

"No one knows this better than you, my dear friend."

After Adia and Tehya had spent time together, they went to find Urilla Wuti and Iella.

"In light of the seriousness of what is going on, I hope you will not take this as being insensitive," Iella said. "But I have some good news. I am seeded."

They heartily congratulated her and assured her

that they certainly wanted to know and share in the joy of the occasion.

"When they return, Moart'Tor can carry the news back to Nootau," Adia said. "We do not know when Pan will return with them, and he should know as soon as possible. But you have both waited this long, so a while longer until you are a family again will hopefully not be any harder than it has been waiting for this wonderful news."

"Do your parents know?" Tehya asked.

"I went to them first. Yes, they are ecstatic."

As they were talking, Apricoria came in. "It is so good to see you both!"

"Urilla Wuti tells us you are a fine Healer," Adia said.

"I am not there yet, but I learn every day. What Urilla Wuti is teaching me is at a deeper level than our Healer, Venturia taught me, and I am happy to be here."

"Moving to Kthama and your coming here has worked out for all of us, "Iella said. "Though I do miss you both, and my parents. But guess what, Apricoria; I am seeded! Nootau and I are having an offspring."

After the congratulatory comments were all offered again, Adia spoke. "Apricoria, Khon'Tor said he had to go after Eitel, the female Sassen who was abducted. Did you tell him that?"

"I saw that both an Akassa and a Sassen had to go

with the Mothoc. This is the one chance to turn the rebels from their ways."

"So you knew that Khon'Tor and the Sassen would be leaving with Moart'Tor?" Adia asked.

"Yes. But I was not given permission to share that. It had to be of their own free will. No soul can command another to risk his or her life.

"Is there anything else you can tell us? Anything you have seen since?" Iella asked.

"I have not been shown anything other than what I shared. Take heart; however, it is always the Great Spirit's will that none shall perish."

A chill crawled up Adia's spine. Those were the same words Moart'Tor had used. Apparently, Adia's face reflected the ominous feeling that had come over her.

"I know," Tehya said. "That statement is where my fear also stems from. There is no question it is dangerous."

"Moart'Tor said there are hundreds and hundreds of the rebels," said Adia. "The only thing protecting Khon'Tor and Eitel's beloved will be the strength of Moart'Tor's words in convincing the rest of the community that neither we nor the Sassen should be killed."

"But even if Pan could not go because of her promise, why would she not send others if there are people of their kind living elsewhere?" Tehya asked.

Adia explained what Moart'Tor had said about

the loss of Mothoc blood and Etera's future if that happened.

"Do not lose heart," Urilla Wuti said. "It does not rest on Moart'Tor's shoulders alone. There is no more powerful orator than Khon'Tor. How many times have we heard him rouse the People at Kthama and comfort them when a threat was near? I would not sell him short."

"You are right. He is a powerful Leader, and hopefully, the Mothoc will recognize it in him," Tehya agreed.

"Come, let us enjoy our time together," Adia said. "Iella and I will be heading back to Kthama in just a few days."

"I have sent a hawk to follow them," Iella explained, "so we may see through its eyes and listen through its ears to what is going on."

"Oh, that is good to hear. Can you tell me, please, what is going on right now?"

Iella found a comfortable spot to enter the silent place within her mind that she had learned was most conducive to connecting with Etera's creatures. Her connection got stronger the more she practiced. And the stronger the connection, the deeper she fell into what looked like a trance state. So she never entered it alone now, always making sure she had company.

Within a few moments, she opened her eyes and reported that they were walking and that all seemed healthy, with no cuts, scrapes, or injuries. Their conversation was mundane, but Paldar'Krah was frustrated with how long it was taking.

They were only a couple of weeks into the journey. Moart'Tor had to slow down to the pace of the others. He could have been much further along if he had been on his own. He knew each day that passed was one more day Eitel was at risk. A fact that was certainly not lost on Paldar'Krah either.

"Can we not travel faster? Perhaps also at night?" he asked.

"The goal is not just to get there," Khon'Tor reminded him, "but to get there in robust health. Not just for our own sakes, should a problem arise, but also for appearances. Both our peoples are smaller than the Mothoc, as you know very well by the size of Moart'Tor here. Arriving run-down and feeble-looking is not going to help our position. And what-ever they are doing with Eitel, another day or so will not matter."

"No matter how strong we appear," Paldar'Krah said, "we are no match for the Mothoc."

"Half the battle is in the mind, Paldar'Krah. If we appear weak to them, they will never see us as worth-while beings. We must arrive with a strong counte-nance on all fronts. Physically, emotionally, and psychologically. Otherwise, we are beaten before we even begin."

"We cannot hope to intimidate them," Paldar'Krah countered. "The size difference alone will settle any hope of that."

"You are not paired yet. Once you are paired, you will understand better how a smaller, physically weaker person can control a larger, stronger one," Khon'Tor replied.

In spite of himself, Moart'Tor laughed. "So true. But that only works because we love our mates. We value them. They are important to us."

"And that will be our challenge here," Khon'Tor said. "To prove our value."

"Forgive me," Moart'Tor countered, "but I cannot imagine my father seeing any value in either of your peoples. However, I am hoping to open everyone else's eyes to realize you are people, just as they are. That your lives are your own, not ours to take. I do realize, though, that in attempting this, you are risking everything to come with me."

"If you cannot convince your father that we have intrinsic value as ourselves," said Khon'Tor, "then we must convince him and your community that we hold value for Etera. Unless we can do one or both of those, we have no chance of freeing Eitel."

He did not need to go any further. They all knew that if Moart'Tor couldn't get through to his father, then even with Moart'Tor's help and the best weapons, they had no hope of rescuing Eitel. Nor did they have much hope of leaving there alive.

Never far from Paldar'Krah's thoughts was what might be happening to Eitel. He wished he could tell her they were on their way. To hold on. He comforted himself with the realization that if they wanted to harm her, they could have done so at Kayerm. They wanted to take her alive; otherwise, they could have killed her there. Why they did not kill Naahb, he could not imagine. Perhaps they panicked, thinking that if they wanted to abduct Eitel, they needed to leave immediately. He had to remind himself that the rebels thought the Ancients were still living among them, which was a huge impediment to their attacking Kthama or Kht'shWea. What had they thought, finding Kayerm empty?

The three of them had just been discussing what value either of their peoples would have to the Mothoc. Of the Akassa, he had no idea. But the Sassen—at least the Sassen females—Paldar'Krah could make a guess. Moart'Tor had shared that their community was running out of pairing choices. Was it possible that that could be the reason Mothoc males would abduct a Sassen female? The thought horrified Paldar'Krah. He calmed himself, remembering that the rebels considered the Sassen abominations. Surely they would never then attempt to breed with one?

Iria was carrying food for wrapped in a large leaf. It was for Eitel.

Kaisak trotted up behind her. "Here, let me take that." Iria handed the bundle to him, and he walked past Gard and down the dark tunnel. He scuffed his feet and cleared his throat, letting her know he was coming. Consideration was not foreign to him. He had learned to become considerate of Visha when he was trying to win her. Now he used it to try to win the Sassen's trust.

"I am bringing you something to eat," he said through the open doorway.

A voice from inside said, "Come in, then."

His eyes had adjusted to the dark tunnel, and he could see her crouched in a far corner. To her right was a sleeping mat in a bit of disarray. A water gourd hung from a protruding rock on one of the walls, dangling by the preserved vine that served as a strap.

He could tell she was watching his every move, so he made sure to move slowly, trying to look as benign as possible. "Would you like me to hand it to you?"

She shook her head and pointed to a spot next to

her sleeping mat. He carefully set it down. "You need to eat. The Healer says so."

He saw her eyes look him up and down, no doubt trying to figure out why the Adik'Tar was bringing her a meal, something any of the females could do.

"I came to apologize," he said. She didn't move, but her eyes stayed trained on him.

"My sons should not have taken you. It was wrong. I sent them there to try to find my son Moart'-Tor. Why they decided to take you from your home, I do not know. They will be punished, to be sure."

She blinked once but said nothing.

"Please, eat. I will not stay long; I only wanted to come and apologize, that is all."

He saw her eyes dart to the food and back. "I am not going to hurt you."

She kept her eyes on him but scooted toward the wadded-up leaf close enough to lean over and snatch it up. She shoved it into her mouth, still not taking her eyes off him. When she was done gobbling it down, she licked her fingers clean.

"Do you want more?"

She quickly shook her head.

"Is there anything else you need before I leave?" Kaisak asked.

"If your sons took me by mistake, then have them take me home."

"It is not as simple as that. First of all, they said Kayerm was empty. So we do not know where home is. Secondly, you are in no shape to make that trip again. Perhaps after you have regained your strength, we can talk about it."

"I know where my home is. My family is missing me. They will come looking for me if I do not return."

"Anything could have happened to you, Eitel. That is your name, right? You could have fallen down a ravine and hit your head. You could have stumbled in the Great River and drowned. They have no reason to think you would be here."

"And how do any of your ideas of what they might think happened to me explain my brother's bloodied body lying outside Kthama's entrance? And your sons were careless. They were in such a hurry to take me that they left the prints of our struggle all over the soft dirt. There is no way my family or anyone there thinks I fell down a ravine."

"What— What do you mean. Your brother's bloodied body?"

"My brother saw your sons holding me against my will. I called out to him to stop and get help, saying that your sons were from the rebel camp. But he kept on running toward us. Your oldest son, Morvar'Nul, hit him. Hard. The last I saw of my brother, he was lying unconscious in a pool of blood. If he lived, they all know where I have been taken. If he did not, the footprints alone would tell them they belong to your kind."

Kaisak rapidly clacked his teeth together, thinking. The look on her face told him the sound was frightening her, so he stopped.

"Rest. I will be back tomorrow to check on you."

Kaisak went directly to find his two older sons.

Morvar'Nul and Nofire'Nul both rose to their feet when they saw their father storming toward them. They looked at each other as if thinking of trying to run away.

Visha saw Kaisak heading there and quickly ran after him.

"What were you thinking?" he roared as he was nearly upon them, his arms flailing about. Visha ran between him and their sons and put both palms up in front of her. "Calm down, Kaisak," she shouted.

"Calm down? Do you know what they did? Do you know the little part they left out about striking down the Sassen's brother?"

"What difference does it make if they forgot to tell you that?"

Morvar'Nul and Nofire'Nul listened to their mother defend them.

"It matters because they did not forget to tell me; they withheld information. They effectively lied to me. Not that I care if there is a dead Sassen somewhere. But when I am not told the truth, that makes me vulnerable. It makes us all vulnerable."

He turned on them, "What else are you not telling me? If there is anything else, tell me now!"

"There is nothing else. I swear." Then Morvar'Nul hesitated and looked over at his brother.

"Except— Except that I tried to mount her," Nofire'Nul confessed.

"Tried? Tried? *Did you*?" Kaisak demanded to know.

"No. But only because Morvar'Nul stopped me. He said it would spoil her, so I left her alone."

"Of all the things I would have understood, that is one of them. I know how hard it is not to have access to a female." Kaisak threw an accusing glance at Visha. "And being on your own with her all that time must have provided a powerful temptation." He was calming down. "So I do give you credit for that.

"But from now on, you will tell me everything. It will go very badly for you if I find you have not been honest. Do you understand?"

Kaisak went to visit Eitel again, this time taking her a handful of lace-dancer blossoms. Gard said nothing but stepped aside from the entrance to let him pass.

This time Eitel must have been stretched out on her sleeping mat as she quickly propped herself up on one elbow the moment he entered her room. He walked toward her. She scrambled away from him, pressing up against the rock wall behind her.

He carefully laid the bundle down and stepped backward. He could see what had to be tear stains on her cheeks.

She looked down at the blossoms but did not pick them up.

"I know it is nothing, really. A silly gesture. I just thought you might like them."

She looked at him with vacant eyes. "What will become of me?"

Kaisak let out a long breath. "Well, I have not yet decided that. I know you want to go home, but that is out of the question. You are here now, among us. Try to make the best of it."

"Are you not the Adik'Tar?" she asked. "Is it not within your power to free me?"

"As I said, it is not that simple. I would like to visit for a while. Why not tell me about where you live. Tell me about Kthama."

"The Fathers-Of-Us-All lived there thousands of years ago. The males lived in Kthama, and the females in Kthama Minor. That is what we were taught anyway."

"Did Moart'Tor visit Kthama when he was there?"

"No. He was only at Kayerm."

"But you said you do not live at Kayerm?"

"No, we do not. My people have not lived there for some time. We only moved back there for a short while—for his sake."

Kaisak was confused. Her answers were abrupt. Perhaps she was still emotionally unstable. "What of the others like him—like us? The Mothoc; did they also move to Kayerm for a while?"

Eitel frowned. "There are no others like you. Except for Moart'Tor, and the Guardian Pan, of course."

Kaisak felt his heart rate increase. What did she mean that there were no Mothoc but the Guardian and Moart'Tor?

"If you have not seen any of us other than Moart'Tor and the Guardian, seeing so many of us together must have been a surprise to you."

"It was."

"Where is Moart'Tor now? My sons went to find him. That is why they went to Kayerm."

"He left with Pan."

Kaisak's patience was wearing thin. It was like trying to quench one's thirst with droplets of water. "To where?"

"We do not know. Somewhere else. There is much about the Guardian that is still unknown to us," Eitel said. Kaisak saw her eyes dart to the flowers and back.

"I cannot give you your freedom yet. Do you understand why?"

"No."

"When Morvar'Nul and Nofire'Nul brought you here, did you notice how the males gathered around you? Until I figure out what is to be done with you, you are safest here."

"Morvar'Nul already said what is to be done with me. I am to be used for breeding. You plan to take all of us from our lives and our families and make us your slaves."

Realizing it was too late to pretend otherwise, he decided to admit it. "It would not have to be that bad if you belonged to the right male. One who would appreciate you."

"If you mean yourself, I have met your mate. I doubt she would take kindly to my sharing your bed."

"My mate and I are estranged. She has no say over my affairs."

Eitel turned her face to the wall, and Kaisak took it that the conversation was over. He did not want to press her. What she had told him already was invaluable. He could hardly contain his excitement. The Mothoc no longer lived with the Sassen. But what about the Akassa? He had to be patient; if he pressed her too hard, she would shut down as she had on the journey with his sons.

"I will visit you tomorrow. If there is something particular you like to eat, let Iria know. I will see if I can arrange it for you."

The Sassen did not say anything in return, and Kaisak left quietly.

When he had cleared the entrance, he stopped and clapped his hands together. The Mothoc no longer lived among the Sassen. Now he only had to find out how many Sassen there were and where they lived.

"Adik'Tar," Gard's voice interrupted his musings. "The Healer Useaves has been asking about you. She would like you to visit her."

Kaisak looked around, realizing Gard was behind him. He should have been out front keeping watch.

"Another time, perhaps," Kaisak answered. *Had Gard been listening to his conversation with Eitel? Perhaps through a little opening in the wall in her quarters?*

Regret filled Eitel after the Mothoc Adik'Tar had left. *I should not have told him all that.* Why had she? The Healer had told her not to tell him anything—or only to tell him a little. What had she done?

She reached over and picked up the bundle of flowers Kaisak had brought her. She held them to her face, breathing in their sweet fragrance and rubbing them lightly over her face, the light tickling sensation pleasing her. She missed being outside.

Eitel was tired of being locked up, though she

understood that, for the time being, it was most likely best for her safety. The stone walls kept her new home cool enough in the late summer heat, just as they did at Kht'shWea. There was a small opening high up on one wall through which sunlight and moonlight reached. She could glimpse a bit of the sky, and at night she could see some of the stars if they were out. Sometimes she would find a small gift up on the sill, no doubt left by Iria or one of Iria's daughters. A piece of fruit, a beautiful feather. A small, brightly colored pebble.

At first, she hoped that someone would come and rescue her, but then, as she calmed down and examined her situation, she realized it would be folly. Even in the brief time when she first arrived, she could see how many and how powerful Kaisak's group was. If Haan did send someone to try to rescue her, they would surely be killed.

She had continued marking the days on a stone Iria had brought her. She dug a little hole in a corner and kept it there, unearthing it each day only long enough to scratch another mark. Sometimes she wondered what the point of it was, yet she still wanted to know. When she did become seeded, and she had no doubt the time was coming, she would use it to figure out when she would deliver.

She thought back to when she was infatuated with Moart'Tor, and how her family had warned her that carrying a Mothoc offling could kill her. And now here she was, going to find out if that were true.

I will not live forever. That was one of the few thoughts that comforted her. No matter what lay ahead of her, at some point, it would end. She would not suffer forever. And she would see her beloved again. And her brother and her family. They would be reunited in the afterlife, and all the pains and shadows of this lifetime would dry up and drift away like leaves at the end of their lifecycle.

Although he did not want to, Kaisak went to see Useaves. He was hesitant to enter as it was late at night. Everyone had since turned in, even Gard, who was usually not far from Useaves' quarters. But he wanted to get it over with.

She was in her quarters, propped up against one of the walls sipping what smelled like willow bark tea.

"Gard said you wanted to see me. What is it now?" he snapped at her. He no longer needed her; she had taught Iria all she could—or all she was going to.

Useaves' voice was weak. "Have you decided what to do with the Sassen?"

"What do you care? What business is it of yours? Leave me be; I am tired of your manipulations."

"My manipulations, as you call them, have gotten you where you are. You would not be Leader if it were not for me." Coughs wracked her brittle frame.

Kaisak scoffed. "I hardly think so. What did *you* have to do with it?"

"Who do you think armed Iria, knowing an attack from Laborn was coming? I knew Laborn had been taking her Without Her Consent, yet no one would have believed her if she told on him. So I armed Iria and convinced her to protect herself. It was the only way to prove what he had been doing to her. I had intended for her only to wound him, to bring to light that he was Taking Her Without Consent. Only, providence smiled, and she killed him."

Useaves had to pause as another round of spasms overcame her. "Either way it turned out, it would have opened the way for you to become Leader. I had originally planned for it to be Gard, but I realized before it was too late that he could never win the people over Dak'Tor. Gard could never have commanded respect, but I knew you could. And so, right after Laborn was killed, I revealed that it was Gard who had hit Laborn over the head and not Dak'Tor, discrediting Gard and leaving you as the only choice for Leader. But in the end, you have turned out to be as short-sighted as Laborn."

"Even if what you say is true," Kaisak snapped back at the old Healer, "what has all this gotten you?

You are no better off than you were the day we left Kayerm. All your lies and manipulation have gotten you nothing."

Useaves swallowed and replied in a raspy voice, "Wrong again. I have gotten everything I wanted. There was no end game for me. There was no objective. What I wanted, I had. Control. Enjoying watching you all fumble around under my influence, leading you one way, then another, as I wished. None of you was a challenge for me except Dak'Tor. He alone seems to have been able to keep one step ahead of me."

"You are insane. There is nothing special about Dak'Tor."

"Dak'Tor is revered among our people, except you are too blind or too arrogant to see it. He is everything you are not. While you focus only on bitterness and anger, he goes among the people and helps them improve their lives. He hunts with the other males. He participates in raising his offling, and he devotes himself to his mate. He teaches all the youngsters skills. He tells stories around the evening fire to entertain parents and offling alike. Where you have set yourself above and apart from them, he has become one of them. I told you long ago that you should gain favor in the eyes of our people, that it was easier to rule the grateful and happy than the resentful and discontented. But you did not listen any more than Laborn did. Given a choice, they would gladly follow him rather than you because you offer them no future."

"No future? I am the one who offers them the only future there is, by breeding the Sassen!" he objected.

Useaves scoffed. "You cannot get away with lying to me. It was not your idea; it was your sons'. I know more about what is going on in this community, even in my sickened state, than you ever will. And as for manipulating others, you are no different than I am. Did you not manipulate Moart'Tor, seeded by Dak'-Tor, raising him to believe it was his mission in life to serve you? You convinced him to use his status to infiltrate the Sassen and Akassa and bring you what you needed to know to carry out your plans against them."

Kaisak ignored her and went on, "You do not know all you think you know. Do you know that our people no longer live among the Sassen? No, I did not think so. And that means we can do with them as we wish. And if breeding with them helps save our people, if that is what gives our people a future, then that is the choice I will make."

"Do you really think the Guardian is going to stand by and let you enslave any of her precious Sassen? Even one of them? Until now, she has left us alone. But your sons, in their short-sightedness, have brought trouble right here to Zuenerth. She could show up at any moment with an army."

"Ancient will not rise against Ancient."

"Are you so sure? Are you willing to bet every-thing on that statement? And as for our people no longer living with the Sassen, do you not think that means they live elsewhere? Do you really believe that we are all that is left of our kind? Look around you. Do you see Etera deteriorating? Do you for a moment believe our own numbers are enough to sustain all of her? No doubt there are more Mothoc and Sassen walking Etera than you could possibly imagine."

She started coughing again. Kaisak glared at her, in her hunched-up state, struggling to breathe. He felt no compassion for her. He hated her. He enjoyed her suffering.

He wondered if Iria or another might come in, hearing her hacking. Yet no one did. It was late, and everyone else was settled down.

"I am leaving. I do not need to stand here and listen to your venom."

Useaves wiped her mouth with her sleeve. "You should. It is not venom; it is the truth. You need to wake up. You are living in a fantasy world where you have everything arranged so you cannot fail, but you need to face the facts. The smartest thing you could do would be to return her to her people and apologize. You cannot win this; you cannot. The males are ready to overthrow you, and then who will take over as Adik'Tar? One of your sons?

Hardly. The people will all turn to the Guardian's brother."

"My own sons? My guards? Never. And why would they? Why would anyone? Besides, Dak'Tor is no different than me; he also believes the abominations must be removed."

"Does he? You speak of it all the time. When have you heard him publicly agree? He stays silent. You really do not know where he stands."

Weakened from talking for so long, Useaves lay back down. "In the end, he's outsmarted us all. He has found favor among the people, and when the time comes that they no longer follow you—and mark my words, it is coming soon—they will turn to him. As for your sons, their taking of the Sassen female from her home, her family, and her life is no different than taking her physically against her will. Your sons have broken Sacred Law, and at some point, the people will realize it. So you see, in the end, your hatred and anger will destroy you and any legacy you might have left."

Kaisak was filled with anger. He wanted only to silence that voice forever. The voice that had taunted him for centuries.

"Well, you will not be here to see it, old female." Kaisak walked over and knelt down. He pinched her nose closed with his fingers and clamped his other hand over her mouth. She was so weak she had no strength to resist.

When he was sure she was dead, he rolled her over and positioned her as if she had been sleeping. He covered her up and left quietly.

Finally, the A'Pozz had bloomed, and Iria spent the day before preparing more of the tincture. Useaves' pain would be eased, hopefully to a bearable level. Although she was obviously dying, there was no way of telling how long she would last, and at least the A'Pozz would help her be as pain-free as possible.

Iria carried the precious preparation and went to Useaves' quarters. The old Healer was still sleeping, facing the rock wall. Usually, by this time in the morning, she would be awake, so Iria knelt down and laid her hand on Useaves' shoulder. It was cold, but then the old Healer was cold almost always now, anyway. "I am sorry to wake you, but I finally have something to help you. Useaves?"

Iria waited a moment and tried to rouse her again. Then she realized the room was quiet. Too quiet. She could not hear Useaves' breathing, which was usually labored, if not even rattling.

"Oh, my," Iria said aloud. She stared at the still body for a moment. "Good Journey, Old Healer. I hope you find peace and forgiveness in the arms of the Great Spirit." She pulled the covers further up over Useaves as if tucking in an offling. She said a quiet prayer and then went to tell the others that Useaves had returned to the Great Spirit.

Useaves' passing was met with mixed feelings. She had been a cornerstone of their community as far back as Kayerm. Some had known her even before then. She was respected for her knowledge but feared for it as well. She had no friends, however. The one closest to her would have been Gard, though he attended to her only out of duty.

Iria helped Gard clean out her living quarters. Her bedding was removed and burned, as were the hides she had used. Iria did not know what to do with Useaves' Keeping Stone as there was no family to leave it with. In the end, Gard offered to take it since he had spent the most time with her of anyone. There was nothing else to remove. Only the cavity in the upper wall remained to be checked, the one that was in each living quarters, a place to keep special items and those that needed to be out of reach of offling. Iria could not reach it, but Gard could. He reached up and back as far as he could into the hole. When he pulled his arm out, he had only a piece of birch paper.

"It has the symbol of your House on it," he said.

Iria unfurled it. Immediately, she knew what it was. The symbols for the antidote that Useaves had never given her. The antidote for Useaves' poison. All this time, Iria had doubted it even existed. She knew this was Useaves' way of saying goodbye.

'What is it?" Gard asked.

"A goodbye message." Iria wiped genuine tears from her eyes.

Kaisak proceeded over the Good Journey ritual. Everyone turned out, partly out of respect, partly out of curiosity. Even Eitel was brought out for it since she was eventually to become part of the community, but Kaisak made sure she was heavily guarded.

"Useaves served us for most of our lifetimes. May she find peace now."

Iria stood a while after the others trailed off. Eventually, she and Kaisak were the only ones left standing. Iria looked up at him and said, "In the end, it was a blessing. Just yesterday morning, she was praying that the Great Spirit would take her. We both knew that even with the help of the A'Pozz plant, there was still a long period of suffering ahead of her. How quickly her prayers were answered."

Kaisak swallowed hard. So Useaves had outsmarted him one last time. She had executed her final manipulation by angering him enough to end her life, sparing her a drawn-out, excruciating death.

CHAPTER 14

Of those Pan brought back with her, Nootau was the one most often seen at Lulnomia. He was a gentle soul and had quickly risen in popularity, regaling anyone who was interested with stories of life at Kthama. In time, he developed quite a following, especially among the older members who had lived among the Sassen and Akassa before coming to Lulnomia. Deep in their hearts, they missed both immensely.

He and An'Kru were both given warmer pelts to wear when needed, as Lulnomia was in a frigid climate - which suited the heavy-coated Mothoc and Sassen very well but certainly not the Akassa.

Nootau tried to hunt to provide for himself and An'Kru, but it turned out to be too difficult in the frigid climate, weighed down as he had to be with so many heavy pelts. As a result, the community met his needs, and Irisa and Rohm'Mok, in particular, made sure he was taken care of.

Instead, Nootau gave generously of what free time he had, meeting with each of the Mothoc communities in turn. He answered their questions about the Sassen at Kht'shWea, and what he knew of the Akassa communities the different Mothoc had left behind. The Mothoc from Kthama were particularly interested in how Takthan'Tor had fared as a Leader. Nootau could tell them only what he knew from their history, how Takthan'Tor's Healer was the first to make contact with the Brothers, and how, out of that, the relationship grew. It was said to have been a slow process, but it was Takthan'Tor's commitment to fulfilling the Rah-hora that had brought the People and the Brothers to the relationship that now existed between them. He told the Mothoc of the new brotherhood that had arisen between the Sassen, the Brothers, and the People and how even a few of the Waschini had become part of their communities.

"The Guardian has told us of the Waschini," someone commented.

"They look like the Brothers, only with lighter skin and more variations of hair color, but their culture is very different. My mother rescued one of their offspring. His name is Oh'Dar, and we were raised together. He is as much my brother as are An'Kru and Aponi."

And that led to other questions, and so it went, with Nootau trying to fill an endless well of curiosity about those the Mothoc had to abandon so long ago.

When he was called to Wrollonan'Tor's world, Nootau spent time with the ancient Guardian himself. Though he would never have the abilities of a Guardian, he had latent talents, which Wrollonan'Tor was helping him develop. One of them was Nootau's ability to receive information directly from the Great Spirit, as Haan did.

"You will never be able to call it at will," Wrollonan'Tor explained, "but we can increase your ability to tune into the vibration through which you receive it." He went on to explain what a vibration was and how the world they were in was just as real as the Etera Nootau stepped into when he headed back to Lulnomia.

"But it is not just as real. It is more real," said Nootau. "It is more beautiful here. Everything is— Is more of what it is back home. It is not as vivid as the Corridor, but it is far more vivid than Etera. And where does all this, everything around us here, come from?"

"I create it. The closer you draw to the Great Spirit, the more in line you are with His will, the more your ability to impact your own reality will increase."

"His?" Nootau's eyes opened wide. "The Great Spirit is a male?"

"No. It is just a term that sometimes makes it easier to refer to The One-Who-Is-Three. The Great Spirit encompasses both the active and receptive traits—which can be thought of as male and female. The active, creative aspect is what allows us to follow our will, to make our impressions on this realm. The receptive nature of the life force allows this realm to accept those impressions, and they can be positive or negative."

"The Great Spirit contains negativity?"

"No. There is only one power in creation, and it is positive and beneficent. But because the feminine aspect of the life force is receptive, negativity in this realm can impact it. And negativity comes from belief in lack, from fear, competition, avarice, and jealousy. But Etera is a slow-reacting realm. If she were not, then all the negative impulses that people have would manifest immediately, and Etera would have been destroyed long ago.

"Look here," Wrollonan'Tor pointed to an area of the glade in which they were sitting. "See that patch of open ground?"

Nootau turned his head. "Yes."

"Push your hand down and move your fist around, then pull it out."

Nootau got up and did as the Guardian said. Then he looked at Wrollonan'Tor for further instructions. Just as he did, a small pond appeared right next to where the open soil had been.

"Now, push that same fist down into the water and repeat what you did before. What is the difference?"

"The soil was barely disturbed compared to the water. And the water responded immediately." Nootau pointed to the circle of ripples expanding out from where he had just removed his hand.

"Very good. Water is a more receptive and fluid medium than the ground. So your action had a greater impact on the water than on the soil. So it is with Etera's realm. Etera's vibration reacts slowly compared to the higher realms. And it is a good thing because, as I said, no one could survive in a medium that was as malleable, as receptive, as say, water, which, when affected, reacts immediately.

"Etera was designed to provide a beautiful home for us while we remain here. We all have the creative life force, so we all have the ability to influence this realm—for good or for bad. But because virtually no one is aligned with the Great Spirit perfectly enough to manifest directly out of the life force, you have to create everything from the materials already in existence in your realm. If you wish to make a basket, you must first collect the reeds, prepare them, cut them to the correct length, then weave them into the pattern. You cannot simply will a basket into existence. So it is with an intention to do something evil. You cannot simply will someone you hate to die; you would have to actively harm them in order to take their life."

"I appreciate your lessons," Nootau said. "I hope it does not turn out to be a waste of your time since I am not a Guardian, and I do not have the abilities any of the others here have. I will never be able to create as you and Pan do and as the Sassan Guardians and An'Kru will be able to."

"Your spirit is impacting your reality already—everyone's is—whether I teach you how to use the ability or not. Of course, your reality is also impacted by the creative power of others—not just through their intentions but also through their actions. While Etera is slow to respond, unfortunately, the Waschini are moving toward a place where their destructive will can immediately be put into far-reaching action. If not stopped, in time, they will develop terrible weapons of destruction. Weapons that can destroy life on an unimaginable scale, even making Etera herself uninhabitable. So our battle to save Etera takes place in both the spiritual and physical realms. But in your time here, my goal is to teach you to align your will, your thoughts, and your heart with those of the Great Spirit. When your alignment draws closer to His, your intentions will become purer and purer, and the creative power of your spirit will strengthen. You are not here by accident, Nootau. And you are not only here to look after An'Kru."

Nootau remembered the conversation he had

had with An'Kru in the Corridor, worrying about what he should do and where he should live. An'Kru told him to trust that he was guided and to have faith that things were unfolding as they should, and afterward, Nootau promised that he would have faith. Now it was time to further fulfill that promise and accept what Wrollonan'Tor said.

Did he regret coming with An'Kru? No. In his heart, he knew he was supposed to be there, only it had not occurred to him that it might also be for his benefit. He and An'Kru had a special relationship, and as hard as it was to be away from Iella and his family, he hadn't second-guessed coming to Lulnomia.

In the evenings, after he and An'Kru had settled down for the night, Nootau would often try to will himself into the Dream World, hoping to see one of his loved ones. But, so far, he had still not been able to make that happen. He made a mental note to ask Wrollonan'Tor about it, as even under Urilla Wuti's tutelage, he had made minimal progress. Perhaps the Guardian could help him develop that ability.

Lulnomia was little different from Kthama or the other Akassa communities, other than it was far colder—enough that he often reached for a wrap. His experiences there frequently made him consider from a different perspective what Oh'Dar's life had been like growing up among the People. Oh'Dar always knew he was welcomed, but he also knew he was not one of them, despite their hospitality and charity.

It was difficult not seeing any other Akassa but An'Kru. Nootau remembered the first time he was among an assembly of the Sassen. Their size had been the biggest shock, and the Mothoc were far larger than the Sassen. When there was an assembly, Nootau kept to the outskirts. Over the years since Hakani and Haan first came to Kthama, and the Sassen had moved into Kht'shWea, he had become fluent in the Sassen language. It was not a difficult progression to the ancient version the Mothoc spoke.

What did help was that Clah, one of the male Sassen Guardians, had taken a specific liking to Nootau and, when free, often sought out his company. Nootau usually bundled up, and they would walk around Lulnomia together at a pace to match Nootau's stride. He assumed it was a bit tedious for Clah to move so slowly, yet Clah never complained. Nootau openly expressed his curiosity about Clah's transition into a Guardian and, in return, answered questions about being one of the People.

Clah and the other eleven had been set on an unexpected journey, which at times, they were even now still learning to accept. When they first saw their reflections, someone else was looking back at them. Their dark locks were gone, replaced by a full coat of silver-white, and the brown of their eyes had been replaced by cold, dark grey, the color of a late-winter storm.

"My mate, Eyota, shared that she often wondered who she was. She was still herself, yet living in a stranger's body. Sometimes she would wake up in the middle of the night and pace about our quarters. I knew she was struggling. We all were, to one extent or another. The vessels we had come to know as ourselves were gone."

"I cannot imagine being changed so in one instant. Have you become accustomed to it by now?" Nootau asked.

"I am less aware of it in myself than I am with Eyota. She is still the mate I loved and paired with so long ago, but physically, she was a stranger to me for a long time. I had to work to see her in the grey eyes that looked back at me. She had to do the same. We all often spoke of it when we were together.

"This was something no one else could help us with," Clah continued. "But there are other aspects of being a Guardian as well. What will it be like to live so long? To see our loved ones, our parents, cousins, brothers, and sisters all age and die. In time, the only constant in our lives will be each other."

"And Pan. And Wrollonan'Tor. And your mates and your offspring." Nootau tried to comfort his new friend.

"Yes. In time, there will be an entire community

of Sassen Guardians as our offling grow and have offling of their own.

"We are the hope of Etera. Although the Aezaitera in our blood is not as concentrated as that of the Mothoc, as our numbers increase, it will balance out. At least, I believe this."

"What is Wrollonan'Tor teaching you?" Nootau asked.

"Through the years, Pan has met with us in the Corridor, and Wrollonan'Tor is picking up where she left off, only deeper and broader. The first step is to recognize our inherent abilities, finding them within ourselves. Can you picture a color you have never seen before? It is like that. Trying to locate a sensation, a field—a zone—that exists within you but of which you have no awareness. Wrollonan'Tor takes us to a salt cave, and we practice there. He is also teaching us to manifest a different reality on a different plane."

"He also spoke to me about that. It is fascinating, really," Nootau agreed. "I wish I had more time to spend with An'Kru," he added wistfully.

"You may feel that you are not doing enough to help him, but trust that you are. Your presence here alone comforts him. I know he usually does not speak like an offling, but he still is one. You are his big brother, and I know he draws strength from your presence. It is difficult to see him as something other than the Promised One, but he has needs just as we do. The quality of the time you spend with him is more important than the quantity. How often we fail to realize that and how much impact we have on each other."

"Thank you for telling me. I know your friendship helps me immensely. From now on, when An'Kru does come back to our quarters, I will make the most of it and stop worrying."

From the day the group had arrived, Rohm'Mok had also taken a supportive interest in Nootau, and so between the two males, Nootau felt he had someone to turn to if he needed advice or an ear to listen to his troubles.

Iella's hawk was ever-present, drifting and riding the currents overhead but never out of sight. Its cries comforted them. At night it lodged in a nearby treetop. Khon'Tor knew Iella could not only see them through the hawk's eyes but could also hear their conversation. And he intentionally spoke to her through it.

They had settled down for the night. "Please tell the others we are doing fine," Khon'Tor spoke to the majestic bird perched overhead. It cocked its head back and forth, listening.

"Moart'Tor tells us Zuenerth is only a few days away. He says their watchers will spot us first, just as ours would at Kthama. So we will rest a few days here before we move on, not wanting to risk coming into their line of sight before we are ready."

Adia and Iella had returned to Kthama, and Iella faithfully passed everything she learned on to the others. How she wished she could speak to the group, yet that was not possible.

Knowing the three travelers were only a few days away raised everyone's stress.

After his conversation with Useaves, Kaisak had decided the safest thing to do was to give the Sassen female to both of his sons to share. That way, he did not have to risk estranging either of them. The community would see the gift as fitting since it was known that the reward for an exceptional act of bravery or service was a female.

However, he could not get over wanting her for himself. After the community was asleep, Kaisak made a habit of visiting Eitel as often as he could. He kept bringing her a treat of some kind, trying to win her favor.

She had a beautiful dark coat and dark eyes, so much like those of Dak'Tor's mate. Many times, Kaisak had entertained himself by thinking of how Laborn had mounted Iria. He could, however, come up with no justifiable excuse for doing the same, and even if he could, Iria was the Healer. Making an enemy of a Healer was a dangerous move. Yes, he had decided to give Eitel to his sons. It was the only way. But he still wanted her, and he had somehow to find a way to have her because his lust for her was starting to consume him. Perhaps he could bed her privately, convincing her to keep quiet about it. If he could do that, no one would know. A fire had burned in his loins all day thinking about it, and he had spent the day quelling his desire for her. But finally, it was dark, and he had his chance.

"I have brought you a present," he said as he entered.

Kaisak had afforded her no right to privacy, so she had no door, and there was no expectation of anyone announcing themselves or asking permission to enter. She was leaning against a rock wall, looking up at the stars through the opening in the roof. She turned when she heard his voice.

He held up a necklace woven from summer flowers. It would not last, of course, but it would stay beautiful for a while. "Let me put it on you." He walked over and slipped around behind her.

She tried to move away, but he put his arm around her waist to stop her. "No, hold still." He leaned in as he placed it around her neck, letting his breath brush over her. He made no attempt to silence his long intake of her scent.

"Please," she said. "Thank you." And she tried to step away.

"Wait, where are you going? Do not move away from me."

"Adik'Tar, please—"

He grabbed her wrist and held it firmly, pulling her around to face him. "I have it all worked out. Tomorrow, I will announce that you will be awarded to my two sons to share in return for their bravery in going to look for Moart'Tor. That way, there will be no quarreling between them. They have always gotten along, and they will work out how to share you."

"What?" she frowned.

"But I am the one you have to worry about keeping happy. They can do nothing for you, but I can. And so, occasionally, I will send them both off on an errand. And then I will show you how a real male takes a female."

When she didn't speak, he said, "It could be a lot worse. There are plenty of males who want you. And they are not all thoughtful like me. Nor would they be gentle. You could do far worse, *Sassen*."

She winced at the term Sassen, and he realized the tone in his voice made it sound like an insult. Or a threat.

"But what about your bloodlines; if you are all sharing me, how will you know which of you has seeded me?" she asked.

"It will not matter. Now that I know my kind is no longer protecting your kind, soon we will have more than enough Sassen females to breed with. Besides, my sons and I share a bloodline, anyway." As he was talking, he was pulling her closer, tightening his arm around her waist. She placed her hands on his shoulders and tried to push him back. He pressed closer. She backed up as much as she could until she was finally hard up against the rock wall.

He saw it in her eyes when she realized her mistake and looked around to see how she might get past him. But he had her trapped, and he pressed himself harder against her, his larger size allowing her no way to escape. He placed one hand over her mouth, and with the other, he reached between her legs and felt around, searching for her entrance.

She started squirming, which made him all the harder. "Be quiet now, or I will make you wish you had been."

Then he placed both hands under her thighs, close to her hips, and lifted her up, so her legs straddled his midsection. He started to lower her, bringing his manhood up against her and feeling the head begin to part her.

Visha's voice broke the silence. "What are you doing? Get away from her!" she screamed. She flew at Kaisak, and he let go of Eitel, who slid down the wall and landed on the floor. Eitel scrambled away on all fours to the farthest point possible.

Visha came at him with claws out. "I knew you were lying, saying you were going to give her to Morvar'Nul or Nofire'Nul. I have seen you looking at her, the same way I have caught you looking at Iria. And I almost believed you when you said you were hoping I could return to your bed."

Kaisak raised his hands to ward off her attack. His mind was in a whirl; he had done it now. He would never be able to safely close his eyes again. "I meant it. I still do. You cannot blame me for this. You refuse to fulfill my needs, so what am I supposed to do, go without forever?"

"And what about me? Does a female not have the same needs? I have gone without satisfaction as long as you have. Yet you do not see me sidling up to another male. You think none of them would betray you by rokking me? You have enemies too. Many of whom would enjoy making a fool of you by mounting me behind your back."

Kaisak now had both her hands at the wrist and was barely keeping Visha from clawing his face.

"I am sorry. I made a mistake," he turned his head to create distance, "I would never have done this if you had left me any hope of returning to your bed! But I see now it was wrong of me, regardless. Besides, tomorrow I will be announcing that the Sassen is being given to our sons as a reward for their bravery in going to look for Moart'Tor."

Holding her still, Kaisak waited for his words to

sink in. He held his breath, vowing to say not one more word until Visha spoke. He kept his eyes locked on hers. He knew that if he even as much as glanced in Eitel's direction, he was as good as dead.

"I have not forgiven you for not sending anyone to look for Moart'Tor," she said, her claws just inches from his face.

Kaisak focused on his own breathing, fighting the inclination to defend himself. "I know," he said. He was watching her closely, knowing he had made a potentially fatal mistake. He had let his desires get the better of him. How had he thought he could get away with this?

Finally, he heard Visha sigh and saw her shoulders drop. He felt the tension in her arms relax, and he knew she was accepting him back. He released her wrists, and her hands dropped to her sides.

He hid his disappointment, knowing now he would never mount Eitel. But just as Kaisak could not risk making an enemy of the Healer, making an enemy of a female like Visha would not have led to a long life either, as was clearly affirmed tonight.

Oh, how he wanted to know how she had found him there. Was it just by chance? Or had she discovered he often went to see Eitel, and to confront him just happened to pick the one night he had decided to mount her?

Or, perhaps, one night, he had not waited long enough for Gard to retire and had passed him in the dark. But what would motivate Gard to tell Visha? Kaisak could not think of anything. He resigned himself to perhaps never knowing what had tipped her off. What mattered now was to put Eitel out of his mind and move ahead with capturing the Sassen and eliminating the Akassa.

He held out his hand to Visha, and she extended hers. He clasped it in his own and led her out of Eitel's quarters with never a backward glance.

Kaisak mounted Visha virtually the moment they got back to what had been their quarters. He was still filled with lust for Eitel and decided he could use it to his advantage to show how much he wanted Visha. After they were done, convinced that all was well between them now, he drifted off to sleep, leaving Visha alone in the dark to think about what had just happened.

Eitel stayed huddled in the corner, stunned over what had occurred. She had come close to being bred against her will. Her treatment since her arrival had proven that these were very different people from the Kht'shWea community. They saw her as sub-standard, not a person at all, just a tool to be used. What would happen to her when she passed bearing age? She had nothing to look forward to now but death.

The next morning, when Iria came to check on Eitel, she found a beaten-down female.

"What happened? Has someone hurt you?" Iria bent down next to her as she huddled in one of the corners.

Eitel turned her face to the wall.

"Talk to me, Eitel, please."

The Sassen just slumped down further, still silent.

Iria waited a moment, then left the bundle of food and a gourd with fresh water in their usual places. Then she sat down a little way from Eitel and said, "I am going to talk to you, and you can just listen; you do not have to respond. I do not know what happened, but something bad did; I can see it in your entire bearing. I know you are sad and depressed, and you have a right to be. I cannot imagine what it is like for you, being taken away from everyone you know and love, and with such a life facing you here as it now appears. But please do not give up hope. Not everyone here is like Kaisak. There are good people here who are just trying to find some happiness under his tyrannical rule. The prior Leader was cold, selfish, brutal. When Kaisak took over, we thought it would be better. And it was for a while, but then as problems started coming up with pairing combinations and the discontent among our people grew, he became angry. As if we were ungrateful for what he had done for us. And it has only seemed to get worse as more time goes by."

Iria sighed. "My mate, Dak'Tor, is the Guardian's brother. I used to dream that we could someday take our family and return to Kthama, where we would be part of a healthy and loving community. That was my heart's desire, but I had to let it go, as it was only making me discontent with my life here. I started focusing on the good I could find. My offlings' laughter while they were playing. A kind word here and there. The beauty of the evening fire lighting up the faces of those I love. I vowed to make peace with the hardships of my life and not let them ruin what joy I could find."

"I am to be given to Morvar'Nul and Nofire'Nul— as a reward for their quest to find Moart'Tor."

"Who told you that?"

"The Adik'Tar. He visited me last night."

"He visited you? To tell you that?" Iria feared what the real reason was.

"Yes. But— No, I should not say anymore."

"You do not have to tell me. I can imagine the rest. But did he get what he really came to see you for?"

"Almost. But his mate interrupted him."

"Visha?" Too late, Iria heard the alarm in her own voice.

"Yes, for a moment, I thought there was going to be bloodshed. But he managed to calm her down. I believe they are back together again."

"Oh, my dear. I am so sorry."

Eitel turned her head and looked at Iria. "Tell me, how bad will it be? Being passed back and forth between them?"

"Not having had a female before, I imagine they will mount you frequently. Nofire'Nul will most likely rush, and it will be over quickly. Of what I know of him, I doubt he will put any effort into making it enjoyable for you. Morvar'Nul is older. He has more sense and will most likely treat you better. In time, the frequency will lessen. Unless one of them starts to care for you, it will most likely just be something to get through, and then it will be over."

"What do you mean, *unless one of them starts to care for me?*"

"If one of them starts to develop feelings for you, then real trouble will start. If it happens, my guess between the two would be Morvar'Nul. At that point, he will not want his brother touching you. He will become protective of you, wanting to keep you for himself. Perhaps even live with you. Nofire'Nul will not want to give you up. There would be a huge falling out. So the best thing for you, no matter how terrible and lonely it sounds, is never to have them see you as a person. Do not let affection blossom. Keep it matter-of-fact. You will be safest if they just get what they want from you and then leave you be."

"They have no right," Eitel said quietly.

"No, they do not." Iria rose to her feet. "Please eat. I will let you know if there is any announcement about your fate."

Useaves' words kept coming up in Kaisak's mind. That the males were ready to overthrow him. And now, he was proposing to award the Sassen female to his own sons. At another time, when dissatisfaction was not high, such a decision would have been touted as the right thing to do. Kaisak had long said that committing an act of valor or considerable contribution to the community was one of the ways to win a female, so his decision would make sense to rational minds. But he was not sure how many of them at this point were still rational.

He took himself as an example. He made a terrible mistake trying to take Eitel—he had known that if Visha found out, she would be furious. Yet he tried to anyway. He let his lust for the Sassen cloud his judgment. He was very lucky Visha had believed he was in earnest when he said he wanted her back, and now he had to live up to it; he would not get a second chance.

Visha was standing at his side as Kaisak got his

older sons together and sat them down. He saw them look at each other, perhaps wondering if their parents had reconciled. He decided to get straight to the point.

"I have decided, as a reward for your going after Moart'Tor and for bringing back a Sassen female, it is only fitting you should get to have her."

Again they looked at each other and then back at him. Almost in unison, they asked, "*You*, who?"

"Which one of us are you talking to?" Nofire'Nul asked.

"Both of you."

"I knew it!" Nofire'Nul crowed. "That is fine with me!"

"I am also happy to share her," Morvar'Nul said.

"Between you, you can figure out how it will work. Only, remember, she is not your mate. She is here to bear offling, nothing more."

"There will be no pairing ceremony then?" Morvar'Nul asked.

"No. Just work out who gets her first and go from there. I have already told her of my decision."

Visha would have been happy for her sons if not for what she had walked in on the night before. She did not blame the Sassen female; she clearly had no choice in what happened to her now. And—to a point—Visha could understand Kaisak's argument that she had denied him and given him no hope of ever being back in her bed. As a result, he had decided to find satisfaction elsewhere. But the Sassen was not *consenting*.

Over the past few days, she had been rethinking the idea of using the Sassen as breeding stock. Visha was a high-spirited female with strong opinions and desires. She had committed her share of spiteful acts, especially against Dak'Tor's mate, Iria, but at her core, she was not an evil person. And as it sank in that her sons had taken Eitel away against her will, and as she put herself in the Sassen's place, it bothered her more and more. And now this.

Without a doubt, her mate was capable of taking a female Without Her Consent. He was no better than Laborn. It did not matter if it was a Sassen or not. And in addition, he was capable of lying to her face. Visha did not for a moment believe her denying of Kaisak relieved him of the responsibility of trying to take the Sassen Without Her Consent. But at the time, she had had to make a choice. Fight him openly and lose her status as Adik'Tar's mate, or pretend to believe him and make the best life she could for herself, so she decided to act as if she believed him and was prepared to take him back. At least she would still be in a position of respect and influence, and her sons would hopefully never have to know their father's true nature.

She also vowed she would never tell Kaisak how she had known where he was that night. Gard had tipped her off, though she had no idea why he would do that. She had never thought he had any loyalty to her—if anything, his loyalty should have been toward Kaisak. But, having seen Kaisak heading that way a few times, Gard had told her of the Leader's frequent visits to Eitel's quarters long after everyone was asleep.

Visha had lost too much in the past few years. Her mother. Her oldest son, Moart'Tor. And now, her faith in Kaisak, both as her mate and as a Leader. She was not going to lose anything more if she could help it.

First light broke over the horizon, gently lighting up the verdant hills and valleys surrounding Kthama. Adia woke and stretched. Acaraho was up and already gone, no doubt meeting with the High Protector about the usual tasks of maintaining the cave system of the High Rocks and other ongoing issues.

She rose and padded over to the food area, looking for something quick she could grab for breakfast. She took some nuts and fresh berries and then went to wash them down with a drink. The water gourd was empty, so she left to fill it herself, knowing how fresh the air was and how pleasant it would be down by the Great River with the day not yet heated up.

As she made her way down her favorite path to the water, a blue bird landed in a tree ahead of her and cocked its head, looking at her first with one eye and then the other. She immediately thought of her mother, as it was a blue bird that had appeared to her just before she died giving birth to Adia. It was not that Adia had never seen such a bird, but this one seemed particularly beautiful. She stopped for a moment to admire and greet it.

CHAPTER 15

It was time. Moart'Tor, Khon'Tor, and Paldar'Krah had risen at first light and were not far from where Moart'Tor said the watchers would see them. The night prior, they had prayed individually and together, asking for Eitel's safety and for wisdom and the words to reach those at Zuenerth.

Moart'Tor believed he could make them listen. He believed they would accept his experience as proof that the Akassa and Sassen were not abominations to be destroyed. He knew it meant going against his father's teachings, yet knowing now how wrong his father was, he had no choice. He had to reach the others.

Paldar'Krah had two goals. One was to rescue Eitel. The other was for all of them to get out of there alive and return to the lives they had left. It was not that he did not care about the Mothoc, but he knew changing their minds lay in the hands of Moart'Tor and Khon'Tor.

Khon'Tor had no illusions about how dangerous this undertaking was. He knew that when evil had taken root in someone's soul, it took near catastrophe to loosen it. It took something so momentous that it shook them out of the delusions intoxicating them. Delusions that wrong was right. Belief in their crusade even if everyone around them disagreed. But he also knew Kaisak did have support and that under tyrannical rule, it was dangerous for those who disagreed to speak out. Dissenters were often vilified and, if the Leader was strong enough, even harmed. It would take a strong majority who already did not agree with Kaisak for this to go the way Moart'Tor believed it would.

Khon'Tor had made peace with his fate the previous night. Not defeat but surrender to the Order of Functions. He was there to do his best, to do what he could. The rest was in another's hands.

They all heard the shouting at the same time. In the distance, four huge figures raised their arms, touting spears. "Those are Zuenerth's watchers," Moart'Tor said.

"No matter what happens," Khon'Tor said, "let your hearts be at peace. What we do here today we do in service to the One-Who-Is-Three."

They kept walking toward the four figures. One broke away and ran off, no doubt to tell the Leader he had visitors. The other watchers waited for them to approach.

As they got closer, one called out, "Moart'Tor! Is that you?"

"Drall!" Moart'Tor called out, recognizing the Watcher. "It is. I have returned. Tell the others!"

The figure waved back, and the rest of the three took off in the same direction as the first.

Khon'Tor's heart was beating hard in his chest. He felt adrenaline surge through his system and instinctively grasped the strap of the lethal weapon he carried. At the same time, he prayed he would not have to use it. As they took the last few steps up to a rise that Moart'Tor said was just at the camp's entrance, Khon'Tor said under his breath, "I love you, Tehya. I love all of our family. Thank you for loving me and for all the days and nights we have shared together."

As they stepped over the ridge, a wall of Mothoc awaited them.

"Moart'Tor!" Visha cried out. Ignoring the others with him, she ran to greet her son. "Oh, by the Mother, you are alive; you have returned. I had given up hope." She threw her arms around him and turned her head to lay it against his chest, and only then really saw the two with him.

"Oh!" she exclaimed, letting go and stepping back.

"You have returned!" Kaisak shouted, stepping through the line of heavily-haired bodies. "And you brought what? Hostages? Prisoners?"

"Neither hostages nor prisoners, Father. Guests. I ask that you welcome them to Zuenerth."

"Guests who come armed?" Kaisak eyed the leather carrier on Khon'Tor's back and the spear in Paldar'Krah's hand. He walked up to the two males and peered down at them, a sneer on his face.

"No doubt you are kin to Eitel?" Kaisak said to the Sassen.

"I am Paldar'Krah; Eitel is my beloved, and we are to be paired. Is she here?"

"She is. Safe. No harm has come to her. And this Akassa?" Kaisak looked to Moart'Tor to explain.

"I am Khon'Tor, former Adik'Tar of Kthama. We have come on a mission of peace. We wish only to take the female Eitel home to her family and loved ones."

Voices murmured, and someone said, "He speaks the dialect of the Ancients!"

Kaisak turned to the crowd and sliced the air with his arm, "Silence!" he shouted.

"May we see her please?" Paldar'Krah asked.

"Not yet," Kaisak answered. "We have some things to discuss first."

Just then, Morvar'Nul and Nofire'Nul rushed up to Moart'Tor.

"Brother! You are well. We went looking for you at Kayerm," Nofire'Nul said.

"Yes," Morvar'Nul agreed. "That is how we found the female Sassen."

Paldar'Krah felt his temper rise. In spite of himself, he started to speak, "And you felt entitled to —" Khon'Tor raised his hand, and Paldar'Krah stopped. Now was not the time to start a fight.

Moart'Tor asked his brother, "Where is she, Morvar'Nul?"

"She is fine. She is being kept in one of the living quarters."

Kaisak stepped between them to end the conversation. "Stop talking; go and stand with your mother."

Dak'Tor was to the right, with Iria next to him. When they had seen who was approaching, Dak'Tor sent their offling back to their living quarters and told them to stay until he or their mother came for them.

"I am Dak'Tor." He stepped forward, addressing Khon'Tor and Paldar'Krah. "I am brother to the Guardian Pan."

"We know her," Khon'Tor said. "I am a direct descendant of your father, Moc'Tor. It is recorded on the Wall of Records housed deep within what was known as Kthama Minor."

"Kthama Minor has been opened?" Dak'Tor had seen the enormous rocks that sealed Kthama Minor.

"Many years ago. It is a long story."

"Who lives there now?" Dak'Tor asked.

"We do," Paldar'Krah answered. "The Sassen live at Kthama Minor, which is now known as Kht'shWea."

"New beginning," Dak'Tor mused aloud, translating it to himself.

Kaisak looked offended that Dak'Tor had taken over, but he was learning what he wanted to know, so he held his peace.

"And you?" Dak'Tor turned back to Khon'Tor.

"The Akassa live at Kthama. We have a peaceful co-existence. There is also a brotherhood, which includes those you knew as the Others. We live in service to the Great Spirit, and we offer you a chance to join us."

"Blasphemy!" Kaisak said, pointing to Khon'Tor yet turning to address the crowd. "For an abomination to speak of service to the Great Spirit."

"They have come a long way, Adik'Tar," Iria spoke up, hoping to appease Kaisak and calm him down by addressing him as such. "Let us at least hear what they have to say."

"Very well. Since you are answering questions," Kaisak said. "How many of you are there, living at Kthama and this Kht'shWea?"

"No doubt you know by now that your kind no

longer lives among us. So the answer to your question is not enough to thwart an attack should you decide to try to annihilate us," Khon'Tor answered.

Many gasped.

"You admit that we could destroy you?" Kaisak said, his eyebrows raised.

"It seems obvious looking at your numbers here. I am not saying we would not defend ourselves, nor that there would be no casualties on your side, but ultimately you would prevail."

"So you come here begging for mercy?" Kaisak scoffed, leaning in. He towered over Khon'Tor.

"We come here, as I said, in service to the Great Spirit."

"And what service is *that*?" Kaisak challenged him.

"Etera cannot survive without Mothoc blood," Khon'Tor said. "Yet your numbers are greatly reduced from the thousands and thousands of Moc'-Tor's time. So Etera is dependent on every drop of Mothoc blood available. From what I understand, you no longer have safe breeding combinations. Etera needs us all, both the Sassen and the Akassa. By annihilating us, you would be destroying your own future, as well as that of your offspring and theirs to come."

"On the contrary. By annihilating you, we would be correcting the mistakes made by Moc'Tor and his brother Straf'Tor. And by doing so, would gain favor in the eyes of the One-Who-Is-Three."

Paldar'Krah was losing his battle to keep quiet. "And how is murdering innocent people an act in service of the Great Spirit?"

"Father." Moart'Tor stepped closer and spoke up. "I have lived among the Sassen. I have come to know them. They are the same as we are. They love their offling, their families. They worship the Great Spirit, just as we do. They wish no one ill will. They want only to live in peace."

"All I hear," Kaisak countered, "is that living with them has poisoned your mind. You can no longer see the truth. You are a traitor."

"He is not a traitor!" Visha shouted, stepping forward to stand in front of Kaisak. "Do not say our son is a traitor! He has come back to us, and we should be rejoicing, not attacking him."

As this was going on, Dak'Tor's followers were unconsciously gathering together behind him. Iria had reached down and clasped his hand. The movement caught Paldar'Krah's eye, and he stared at them for a long time.

Gard stood to the far side with the guards, who had their spears in hand. As the voices started rising, mothers were taking their offling from the center to the periphery of the crowd.

Khon'Tor addressed Kaisak, "You are the Leader. Surely you want what is best for your own people?

Our existence is no threat to you. We are no different than you. We worship the Great Spirit. We are very much like those you called the Others, who were once your wards and under Mothoc protection. If we come from them, how can we be evil? The Sassen and my people carry not only your blood in our veins but also that of the Others. So why would your protection not extend to us as well?"

"Do not preach to me of my own history! What do you know of it?" Kaisak bellowed. He stepped even closer to Khon'Tor and was now yelling in his face.

Khon'Tor did not flinch as he held his ground.

Kaisak raised his voice even louder, "Moc'Tor and Straf'Tor betrayed the very ones who were ours to protect. The Others!"

"Adik'Tar 'Tor knows much of our past," Paldar'Krah said. "The entire history of Wrak-Wavara is recorded on The Wall of Records, buried deep within Kthama Minor. Not far from the tomb which holds the bodies of Moc'Tor, Straf'Tor, and E'ranale."

The members of the crowd could contain themselves no longer. Remarks were made about the Great Spirit entrusting the Sassen and Akassa with such treasures and ancient secrets.

Kaisak shouted over everyone, "Enough. Do not listen to them; they will say anything to turn you against me."

"Our purpose here is only for peace," Khon'Tor

said. "While yours is to deprive your people of the truth—and to deprive us of the lives given to us by the Great Spirit."

"You and your kind should never have been created. You are an abomination, and it is given to us to wipe you from the face of Etera," Kaisak said.

"Our blood carries the same life force as yours. Other than our appearance, we are no different from you," Khon'Tor said. "Our different physical traits do not make us an abomination."

As he spoke, Dak'Tor was studying him closely.

Moart'Tor raised his voice to address the crowd. "Nothing created by the Great Spirit can be an abomination. Abomination comes from the evil we harbor in our hearts and what we choose to do. The evil we do; that is the abomination. If you could know them as I do, there is no reason for the Great Spirit to want them destroyed. If you believe, as my father says, that Moc'Tor and Straf'Tor betrayed their wards, the Others, then you would be doing the same thing by harming the Akassa and the Sassen since the Others' blood flows in their veins. They have come here offering peace, offering you the same brotherhood they share between themselves and the Others. Yet my father says they all deserve to die?"

Kaisak motioned to his guards, who raised their spears and surrounded the three.

"I have heard enough of these lies," he shouted. "I will hear no more talk of how the Akassa and

Sassen are just like us. But my eyes have been opened further. It is not enough to cleanse Etera of the Akassa and the Sassen; the Others must also be killed. That way, there will never be the temptation to breed with them again.

"As for you," Kaisak looked at Moart'Tor. "I will demonstrate how we treat traitors. You will be executed alongside the Akassa and Sassen atrocities you have brought to our village."

"You cannot!" Visha grabbed Kaisak's shoulders and forcibly turned him to face her. "You cannot execute our son. From the time you started pursuing me, you promised both me and my parents that you would love him as your own. How can you say you will have him killed?"

"Well, he is not my son, now, is he?" The viciousness in Kaisak's eyes was no longer veiled.

Visha stumbled backward but was caught by Morvar'Nul and Nofire'Nul before she could fall. As they helped her upright, she saw her father approaching from behind.

"You deceived us," Visha's father, Krac, said. "And you deceived Visha too. I believed you when you asked permission to pair with our daughter and vowed to raise her son as your own."

Dak'Tor walked to the front. "What you say is true, Kaisak. No, Moart'Tor is not your son. He is mine. And I am proud of him. You heard Moart'Tor and the Akassa Leader. They speak with true hearts.

Look at them as they stand before you now; the Akassa and the Sassen are just like us. What difference does it make if they look different? Anyone can see that our blood, as well as that of the Others, flows in their veins."

Dak'Tor pointed at Kaisak. "I will not stand by and let you slaughter innocent people because of your hatred and prejudice."

Useaves was right. He cursed her under his breath.

"Listen to me," Dak'Tor addressed the crowd. "If he can do this to Moart'Tor, whom he raised as his own, what more will he do to you? Or your offling? Who will stand with me against tyranny and hatred?"

A male shouted, "Not all of us believe the Akassa and the Sassen are abominations."

More and more people chimed in until there was a cacophony of voices, all running together, rebelling against Kaisak.

"You have lost, Kaisak," Dak'Tor said. "All your years of spewing hatred and malice cannot prevail against the truth. They can see that the Akassa and Sassen are their blood too. Your people have had enough of your lies."

"Hear me, Zuenerth," Moart'Tor shouted above the din, which then immediately stopped. "You do not have to live like this, struggling to find resources, with no joy in your lives other than what you can scratch out day to day. There is a thriving community of Mothoc living in a place called Lulnomia. All the remaining Ancients who left Kthama—and all the other Akassa and Sassen communities—live there with their offling and their offling's offling, as far back as you care to count. It is where I have lived since I left Kayerm. Pan has declared that you are welcome. You are welcome to live out your lives in peace, surrounded by thousands of your own kind. Friends, perhaps even family who the eldest of you left behind at the time of the great division. Your offling would grow up to find mates and have families of their own."

Many in the crowd gasped at hearing there were thousands of other Mothoc existing somewhere else.

At hearing his sister's name, Dak'Tor's eyes darted quickly to Moart'Tor. Lulnomia. He had briefly heard his sister speak of it. It was the location they were preparing to go to after they left the Akassa and the Sassen.

"But you cannot come with hatred in your heart. Hatred and distortion were created by Norcab, then continued by Ridg'Sor and Laborn. And now the male whom I called father," Moart'Tor looked at Kaisak, sadness filling his eyes.

"The Guardian Pan offers you a new life," Khon'Tor said. "Among your own kind."

"You heard them!" Dak'Tor shouted. "We can go home. They speak of the community led by my sister,

Pan. They are waiting for us. Waiting to welcome us. It is true. It does exist. I heard of it before I left Kthama." He flung his arms wide as he spoke. "Who will join me at Lulnomia?"

A nearly deafening din of voices rose up, proclaiming that they wanted to go with Moart'Tor and Dak'Tor to Lulnomia. Iria looked up at her mate with hope in her eyes.

"Yes, take us with you. There is no future here," one voice called out. Others joined in, arms waving and many of them turning to each other in astonishment. Only Kaisak's guards remained unmoved.

"No one leaves!" the Leader bellowed. He stormed over to one of the guards and grabbed the huge spear from his hands, and charged Dak'Tor. Overhead a hawk let out a piercing cry.

Dak'Tor dodged the spear and then engaged Kaisak in the fight of his life, trying to tear the weapon from Kaisak's hands. The guards roused themselves and started to intervene, but before they could, Dak'Tor's followers rushed forward and engaged them in battle.

Visha was frozen to the spot, witnessing the horror breaking out before her, the rip of powerful claws and glistening canines tearing at flesh.

The terrorizing howls and growls caused all wildlife in the area to flee. Birds took to the air in droves while deer and other creatures scattered in all directions. Blood splattered everywhere, and huge bodies crashed into the landscape, uprooting and felling entire trees and groves on impact. Dak'Tor's followers were unarmed; it was nothing less than slaughter.

In the background, some of the mothers and other females fought viciously to form a line behind which yet others rushed the offling inside to safety.

Visha prayed to the Great Spirit for help. For intervention.

Then, remembering Eitel, she ran to get her. Though she was safer where she was, Visha felt she should know what was happening and at least know that her friends had come to rescue her.

Visha slammed into the sides of the tunnels as she hurried to Eitel's room.

Hearing her, Eitel stepped outside her doorway. She could hear the commotion outside.

"What is happening!" She wanted to leave her confines but was also afraid of what was going on.

"Moart'Tor, with an Akassa and your beloved," Visha said, panting, "have come to rescue you. But a fight has broken out between my mate and his followers and Dak'Tor and his. Apparently, all this time, Dak'Tor did not agree with Kaisak about annihilating the Akassa and your kind.

"Paldar'Krah is here? He came for me after all!"

At that moment, Visha no longer saw Eitel as a Sassen. She saw her as a fellow female, one who had the same desires and longings as she did. All the things the Akassa Leader had spoken of. All the things they struggled to find here at Zuenerth but that were freely being offered at Lulnomia.

"Moart'Tor said there is a place called Lulnomia, that the rest of our kind live there, all those we left behind when we left Kayerm, the followers of Moc'Tor and Straf'Tor alike. Moart'Tor has been living there since he left Kayerm with the Guardian. He is offering my people a chance to return with him, to live in a thriving, peaceful community. Only, my mate will not let the people go. Oh, Eitel, it is terrible. It is terrible; there is blood everywhere. They are all killing each other."

"Take me to Paldar'Krah, please. I would rather die at his side than live a lifetime of captivity."

Visha scurried outside with Eitel in tow. The Sassen's hand flew to her mouth when she saw the slaughter going on before them.

Visha quickly scanned the frantic motion and flinging carnage, then she dragged Eitel around one side, as far away from the commotion as possible. She spotted Gard, a way off with about ten of his males. They were standing in a circle, a nearly solid wall of Mothoc bodies. Somehow she knew, inside that circle, they held the Akassa Leader and Paldar'Krah captive. She wondered if Moart'Tor were among them.

The two females wove their way to the guards. When they were halfway there, Eitel heard

Paldar'Krah call her name. She hurried as fast as she could along the rest of the perimeter, skipping and dodging the bodies between her and her beloved. Gard, who was part of the circle, stepped aside, creating an opening and letting her in.

Paldar'Krah grabbed her and pulled her into the protective center of their group.

"You came for me," she cried out. "I prayed that you would. And that you would not. I feared this very thing happening.

"I have lived to see you again, and I will forever be grateful for this gift," he replied.

"But why, oh why, would you come? You have seen Moart'Tor and the Guardian. You had to know you would stand little chance, the two of you, against Kaisak's army. Even with Moart'Tor's help."

"We were going to come anyway. We were not going to let you be taken away without trying to free you. Moart'Tor came to help us and to try to convince his people there was another better life waiting for them if they could just set aside their hatred."

Moart'Tor looked down and said, "Forgive me. I thought they would listen."

"They did," Visha said. "They listened to all of you. Did you not hear their voices? They turned against Kaisak. More than half of Zuenerth shouted that they wanted to go to Lulnomia, but Kaisak would rather murder them than let them go."

The commotion began dying down but only because there were few left to fight. Gored bodies lay strewn everywhere, and the ground was red with blood. Those still alive were moaning in pain. Only a handful remained fighting.

No longer hearing the shouting and screaming, and with the offling safely inside, the females began poking their heads out before gingerly stepping outside. They moved quickly from body to body, stooping down, looking for their mates, fathers, sons, and brothers. The stench of blood was everywhere. Wails of grief joined the moans of the wounded as they found dead family members. Females bent over their fallen loved ones, crying and hugging their bodies. There were a few happy reunions, those not fatally wounded, who had escaped a second spearing to finish them off. But these were few and far between.

Iria knew there were some survivors as she could hear them moaning. Both her grown daughters had come out to help, Lurir, who was being trained as a Healer, and Nakai.

She scanned the carnage, desperately looking for her family. She found her oldest son, Isan'Tor, her firstborn, dead. Blood stains were splattered over his silver-white back and head, markings so very much like his father's. She looked over the other bodies, terrified she might find her younger sons among them. They were not among the dead, but there were far too many Mothoc who were.

Finally, she called out to her daughters, "Isan'Tor is dead! Do you know where the others are?"

Nakai called back, "All three are safe inside, with the other offling."

The tiniest relief spread through Iria's heart for a moment, but then the loss of Isan'Tor flooded back over her. She wanted to give into her grief but knew she had to go on, so she shoved her feelings as far down as she could. There would be thousands of years to mourn their son. She looked next for Dak'-Tor. She found him, wounded but alive, with Kaisak's bloodied spear lying by his side.

She rested his head on her lap and quickly examined his wounds. Miraculously he was not fatally wounded. He rolled over on his side and then sat up. He wiped blood from his eyes and face and looked around.

"Where are our offling?"

Iria shook her head. "Isan'Tor is dead. Lurir and Nakai are helping the wounded, and from what I can tell, the others are safe inside. Some of the females hurried all the offling to safety the moment the fighting broke out."

"And what of Moart'Tor, Khon'Tor? The Sassen male?" he asked.

"I do not know," she answered.

Dak'Tor pulled himself to his feet with Iria's help. Most of his followers lay dead. Dazal, his dearest friend. Iria's father. Nearly all the adult males who had joined the battle were gone. They had been unprepared and unarmed, easy targets for the guards. It had all been for nothing. In the end, Kaisak had won after all.

Kaisak had scrambled to safety after stabbing Dak'Tor, but now returned, arrogant and even more energized. Some of his guards were suffering from deep gouges and bite wounds, while some nursed broken limbs, but only one or two were dead. He ordered those living to the front.

"Come around, people of Zuenerth!" he shouted. Slowly the rest of the females came out, along with some of the younger males who had retreated with them. The guards, watchers, and several other males also gathered around, stepping over bodies as they came together.

"Behold, followers of Dak'Tor. This is the result of your listening to his lies. This is the doing of the Guardian's brother and his followers. The Great Spirit has judged them, and they have paid the price for their misguided beliefs."

Then Kaisak saw the group surrounded by Gard and some others. "You captured them," he said.

"Good." Visha, Dak'Tor, and Iria were among them. Lastly, he saw Eitel in the arms of the Sassen male.

"How touching," he taunted them. "And how nice of you to assemble together. That way, you will have a clear view as I execute each of you, one after the other."

"Spare my mate," Dak'Tor said. "She has done no wrong."

"I will gladly spare your mate," Kaisak said. "But you will watch your friends die before you do."

"If you kill him, I will never help you again," Iria growled.

"Then I will make you and your daughters wish you had died with him."

Iria looked up at her beloved, who leaned down and whispered something to her. She looked up at him with tears in her eyes. "I love you so much. You have been my world. I will do as you ask and go now. We are bound together in ways that death cannot touch."

The circle parted to make way for her to leave. She turned back to look at her mate once more, then hurried away.

Kaisak stood in front of Moart'Tor. "Not a scratch on you; you did not fight? Have I raised a coward?"

"Mothoc will not rise against Mothoc. That is what you taught me."

"Well, apparently, I was wrong." Kaisak looked at

his mate, standing with the Outsiders. "Step outside of the circle. Step away from him if you want to live."

Visha stood still, lifted her chin, and crossed her arms. "There are some things worth living for. And there are some things worth dying for. It is up to each of us to decide which is which."

"Very well, then. Moart'Tor, for your treason, you will be the first to die." Kaisak quickly grabbed the spear out of one of the nearby guard's hands and started to jab it toward Moart'Tor. Visha screamed and flung herself in front of her son. Kaisak's blade pierced her directly through the center. Her body convulsed, curling around the spear and dragging it with her out of Kaisak's hands to the ground. A current of blood gushed, and she cried out in pain.

"Mama!" Moart'Tor collapsed over his fallen mother. Kaisak grabbed another spear and drove it into Moart'Tor's back.

Moart'Tor moaned and rolled over, reaching back to try and pull out the spear. Kaisak swiftly grabbed another and finished him off, also piercing his body through the center.

Before he closed his eyes for the last time, Moart'Tor turned his head to see his mother lying beside him, still.

Morvar'Nul and Nofire'Nul both screamed, "Nooooo!"

Vollen'Nul ran over to Morvar'Nul and clutched him around the waist. Morvar'Nul bent over and covered his eyes, so his youngest brother could no longer see the still bodies of their fallen mother and brother.

Nofire'Nul charged his father, yelling, "You killed Mother. And Moart'Tor. You are evil. You are the abomination! You are the one who must be destroyed."

Kaisak reached out to grab another spear, but Gard shouted, "No, no more!" and stepped in front of the Leader. "I can no longer stand by and let you continue to hurt others!"

They struggled, and within moments, Gard joined the others on the ground, his life oozing out of him.

"Where is Iria?" Kaisak bellowed. "She must be here to see her mate receive his judgment!"

Heads turned to look for her, but she was nowhere in sight.

Iria had left as Dak'Tor asked her to. She knew what she had to do. They had discussed it enough times, on the outside chance that something like this might happen one day. She hurried down the tunnel to their quarters, where she quickly pulled a rock over to the far wall and climbed onto it. She felt for the hidden seal, the plug of the secret cavity Dak'Tor had so carefully fashioned as to be invisible. She felt the edges and clawed it out. Then she reached back and felt around with her hand. Her fingers clasped the precious item that Dak'Tor had stored there thousands of years ago.

She pulled out the sacred crystal. Dak'Tor had wrapped it in a small piece of soft hide, and she remembered his instructions.

"Saraste', only when all hope is lost are you to complete this most important task. The crystal is of unknown power. It was hidden in the 'Tor Leader's staff for eons. Whatever happens, it must not fall into the hands of Laborn and his ilk. We cannot take the risk that they might figure out how to use it. If all is lost, It must be destroyed, even if it takes our last breaths to do it."

She stepped down off the rock and placed the crystal on it. Then she picked up another rock and brought it down, shattering the crystal into a thousand pieces. She scraped the largest bits into the center of the stone and smashed them again and again until there was nothing left but small shards and dust. Then she dug a hole in the floor, scraped in the remains, and used the rock to hide it.

By now, tears were streaming down her face. She turned and leaned against the wall, her heart heavy with unbearable grief. She was only there a short while before two of Kaisak's guards came and hauled her out.

"You are to witness your mate's death. Kaisak's orders."

Iria struggled but to no avail as they dragged her to where Kaisak was waiting. She turned her head at the sight of the limp bodies of Moart'Tor and Visha lying close to each other.

Kaisak picked up the spear he had used to kill Gard and started moving menacingly around the guards encircling Khon'Tor, Dak'Tor, and Paldar'Krah, who still had Eitel in his arms. With his hand on the sheath of his weapon, Khon'Tor's eyes never left Kaisak. However, everyone was too close to risk using it. Khon'Tor had to wait for his moment.

Then Kaisak held out his hand and motioned to Paldar'Krah, "Give her to me."

"No," Paldar'Krah said.

"Give her to me if you want her to live." Kaisak raised his hand, and the Mothoc guards moved to let him enter the circle.

Kaisak was now only a few feet from the prisoners. He started laughing. "You think you can escape your fate? Look at you. Look around you. You are going to die. All of you. But as for you," he said to Paldar'Krah, "your only choice is whether she lives without you or dies with you."

Paldar'Krah looked down at Eitel, "Go with him. At least you will be alive."

Eitel wrapped her arms tightly around him. "No. If I cannot live with you, then I choose to die with you. We will be together in the afterlife. Not even he can prevent that." She turned her head to see where Kaisak was but couldn't see him.

Just then, Paldar'Krah gasped and shuddered. Eitel looked down to see the tip of a spear protruding from his torso. It had narrowly missed piercing her as well. Kaisak pulled the spear out, and Paldar'Krah collapsed to the ground.

With lightning speed, Khon'Tor pushed Eitel out of the way and grasped the weapon Awan had made him so long before. He stood off against Kaisak, who motioned to the guards to stay out of it. They widened the circle so the two could fight. Eitel ran past them to where Iria was being restrained.

"Of all the evil souls I have encountered in this lifetime," Khon'Tor said, locking his gaze on Kaisak, "yours is the darkest. You have destroyed your own community and caused the slaughter of innocent people. Your sons will never forgive you. You think you have won, but you have lost. Everything."

They continued to circle each other. Kaisak had the distinct advantage of size, whereas Khon'Tor had the advantage of agility.

Dak'Tor was off to the side, watching, his fists clenching and unclenching. He could see Iria still being securely held, so she could not intervene.

"Stop it!" Iria called out. "Stop it!" She twisted in the guards' grip.

In the next moment, one of the guards tossed his

spear to Dak'Tor, who entered the fight. Now both he and Khon'Tor sided off against Kaisak.

Kaisak glanced up and saw who had thrown Dak'Tor the spear. "Salus, your loved ones will pay for your treason."

Salus laughed, "And who would that be? My daughter is already dead, as is her mate, Krac. Both are lying dead because of you. I have little left to lose."

"Look around, Kaisak," Dak'Tor said. "The army you created to destroy the Akassa and the Sassen is no more. You have your guards, but you do not have enough males left without those of my followers who lie wounded before us. It is over. A moment ago, I thought you had won. But you have failed."

"Since I am still alive, and you will not be in a moment, I hardly see that it is I who have failed. And where is your precious Guardian sister? The one everyone told me to fear. I do not see her coming to your rescue!"

Pan had learned long ago to live deeply in the present, blocking out the otherwise continual impressions she received from others. If she did not, the constant distraction made it impossible to think, let alone hear the voice of the Great Spirit."

Wrollonan'Tor called her to him. "You need to

know what has happened at the rebel camp. Moart'-Tor, the Akassa Leader, Khon'Tor, and Eitel's beloved reached Zuenerth. They were immediately captured. An uprising broke out. Nearly everyone is dead."

"My brother?" Pan could feel the blood draining from her face. Her heart was pounding.

"He will last but a moment longer. His mate and daughters are still alive but, as a result, face a difficult life ahead."

"Why would the Order of Functions allow this?"

"You know the answer. The Order of Functions does not control events. It can only react to what happens, what the free will of others creates. It is constantly readjusting, trying to bring the best outcome out of every circumstance, trying out an infinite number of combinations in a mere flash of time as we know it. Sometimes, the best outcome is a term beyond our understanding."

"My brother is about to die, all because of the free will of evil people. If I had known, I would have gone—" Then she remembered her promise to Adia never to leave An'Kru. She could not have gone. She turned to see An'Kru standing a short distance away, watching and listening.

"You need to know that Dak'Tor never betrayed you," Wrollonan'Tor continued. "All these years, he kept the existence of the crystal a secret. When it became obvious that death was imminent, his mate Iria destroyed it, lest it fall into the rebel's hands."

The sick feeling in the pit of her stomach became worse. "The crystal is destroyed. My father will never be free from the vortex." As despair overcame her, she sagged against the nearest wall.

Finally, she asked, "Moart'Tor? Khon'Tor?"

Wrollonan'Tor shook his head.

"How am I to tell Naha that her mate is gone, that her offling is fatherless? She will have to raise Akoth'Tor alone, and as much as we love our offling, they cannot replace a mate!"

Khon'Tor and Paldar'Krah both knew Kaisak could outlast them. Even with Dak'Tor's help, they had no illusions about their fate. And they had no illusions about Kaisak's drive to win, no matter the cost. All they could do was somehow fatally wound him before they fell.

Paldar'Krah glanced briefly at Eitel, huddled as close to Iria as she could get. Then he glanced at Khon'Tor. "Ready?" he asked.

Paldar'Krah charged Kaisak from the front, and Khon'Tor moved in from the rear, swinging his deadly weapon in wide arcs. The tip of the spear touched Kaisak, and the obsidian at the end carved an angry wound across his lower back. Kaisak cried out in pain, and Paldar'Krah rushed forward and stabbed Kaisak while he was still reeling from Khon'-

Tor's wound. But his angle was off, and the blade entered relatively harmlessly. He was about to slash at the Leader again, but Dak'Tor rushed forward and managed to puncture Kaisak's other side.

Blood was spreading from his wounds, and Kaisak stumbled but did not fall.

Adrenaline energized all the fighters, and their senses and reactions were at the highest level possible.

"Kill them!" Kaisak yelled at his guards, his hand covered in blood as he clutched his side. The spear in his other hand clanked to the ground.

Other than Salus, who had tossed his spear to Paldar'Krah, the Mothoc males closed in. Khon'Tor and Paldar'Krah were once again surrounded by a wall of gigantic hair-covered bodies. One reached out and struck Khon'Tor in the face, knocking him to the ground. Another grabbed Khon'Tor's weapon and swung it at the Akassa. The weapon was expertly made, doing its job regardless of who yielded it. Khon'Tor cried out as it entered on one side and sliced through to the other, leaving a gaping wound of bloody flesh and nearly cutting him in half. A river of blood gushed from his midsection. Meanwhile, two of the others struck down Paldar'Krah and ran him through. Dak'Tor fought for his life with his last bit of strength, but in the end, he was outnumbered. As he breathed his last breath, he said, "Forgive me, sister. Forgive me, Mother and Father. Great Spirit, please look after my—" And he was gone.

Khon'Tor was still alive but barely. He felt no pain, but he could feel himself tiring. He knew he was dying. His last thoughts were of his beloved Tehya and his daughter and son, whom he would not be there to raise. Of all the moments that had made up his life, good and bad, which would he be remembered for, he wondered. He thanked the Great Spirit for his blessings and again asked forgiveness for his failings.

The cry of the hawk overhead was the last sound he heard.

At Kthama, Iella had seen and heard it all. She was deep in a trance, leaning against an oak with her head back and eyes closed, and, cut off from the outside world, was connected with the hawk that flew over Zuenerth.

She had been in and out of the hawk's mind while Moart'Tor, Khon'Tor, and Paldar'Krah were making their way to the rebel camp, and she had given the others updates while also tending to other duties. And although nothing noteworthy had happened then, this day was different. Since morning, when she made the connection, she had not yet come out of it. She was agitated, at times wincing, at other times nearly crying out.

Those watching were helpless to intervene, not knowing if it would break the connection and whether it could be restored, and whether it would harm her to do so. But they knew whatever Iella was seeing and hearing was deeply troubling.

Finally, Iella came to and immediately fell forward, sobbing. She started rocking herself back and forth. "No, no, no!" she cried.

The others around her rushed to her side.

"What is it? Are you alright? Please speak to us," Adia pleaded.

Iella rolled over onto all fours and crept along the forest floor, moaning and sobbing. Finally, she collapsed and lay face down, saying over and over again, "No, no, no." She clawed at the ground in anguish, pulling up tufts of moss and soil.

Adia, Nadiwani, and Acaraho quietly stayed near, giving Iella time to collect herself. The three looked at each other, their eyes filled with silent pleas that what they feared most had not come true.

"They are all dead," Iella finally said. She rolled onto her back, her hands still covering her face. Huge tears rolled from her eyes and soaked into the forest soil below.

"They are all dead. Slaughtered. Every last one of them. Khon'Tor. Paldar'Krah. Moart'Tor. Even the

Guardian's brother, Dak'Tor. The Leader murdered them all. Carnage everywhere."

"All of them? Oh, by the Mother, please say it is not true," Adia gasped.

"Eitel. She is still alive, as is Dak'Tor's mate. But it would be better if they had died as well. Their pain and suffering are unbearable."

All of Zuenerth, those still alive other than Kaisak's followers, were devastated at the scene before them, almost to the point where they could no longer function. Most of the survivors were females and offling, and there was crying and moaning everywhere.

Kaisak lay on the ground looking over the bodies of his enemies at Khon'Tor's bloodied weapon, which lay discarded. In the background stood his sons, looking at him with blank faces.

The guards holding Iria had let her go, and she and Eitel had fallen to their knees, their arms around each other as they wept.

What, a day before, had been a community of hundreds was now culled down to a third of its former size. Gone were Kaisak's plans to destroy the Akassa and the Sassen. Without Dak'Tor's followers, who were nearly all dead now, Kaisak would not have enough males to stage his attack. Though he now realized he had never had their allegiance.

Iria looked for her daughters and found the two oldest again moving among the wounded, trying to help whoever they could. She said a prayer of gratitude that they had been spared, though she had lost both her mate and Isan'Tor.

She slowly rose to her feet and helped Eitel stand. Then she looked at the crowd of females. She was looking for her mother and briefly closed her eyes in thanks at seeing her cradling a young offling —Iria's youngest daughter.

Iria knew she must somehow look away from what she had lost and look forward to what she still had.

The females gathered together, those who were unencumbered taking each others' hands. They bowed their heads and began praying the most ancient of their prayers, and they swayed together as they lifted their voices to the Great Spirit. They prayed the prayer of forgiveness. They prayed the prayer of intercession, asking for help for all those who had survived. They prayed for healing, not just of the bodily wounds but for the emotional wounds, which would far outlast any physical damage. Slowly, those of the wounded who were still able to stand joined them. Iria's daughters, Lurir and Nakai, stopped what they were doing and also joined in prayer. Even Morvar'Nul and Nofire'Nul came over.

Of the living, only Kaisak and his die-hard followers did not join the prayer circle.

Kaisak made it to his feet; his many wounds seemed to be superficial. He stood over the bodies of Khon'Tor, Paldar'Krah, and Dak'Tor. He kicked Khon'Tor's body, rocking it and making sure the Akassa was dead, even though, from the wound which ran from one side to the other, there could be no doubt. Then Kaisak walked over to Dak'Tor and smiled down at his lifeless form. As for Paldar'Krah, the Leader took no notice of him. He was only a stranger trying to save his female, and Kaisak was indifferent to his death.

Blood was running down his face, and he wiped it off with the back of his hand. Then Kaisak looked across at the remaining guards and his loyal follow-ers. Perhaps thirty or so. As far as he knew, none of the females or offling had been harmed, and for that, he was grateful. But with so few males to hunt for everyone left, starvation was a likely possibility.

Acaraho carried the news to Kthama. Disbelief spread through the crowd and was followed by grief. Those standing knelt and began praying. Those sitting bent their heads in prayer.

Haan's people were in mourning, too. Eitel and Paldar'Krah's mothers tried to console each other while the fathers stood silently by, dealing with their loss in their own way. The same ancient prayers that were filling the air at Zuenerth were also being chanted at Kht'shWea.

As the voices of those in prayer filled both Kthama and Kht'shWea, Adia came to speak with Acaraho.

His face was lined with pain. "I should not have let them go. I should have stopped them. The odds were too highly against this succeeding."

Adia placed her hand on her mate's cheek to make him look at her. "There is nothing you could have done to stop them. They would have gone anyway. None of it is your fault."

In a choked voice, Acaraho said, "In the end, Moart'Tor proved true to his word. He did his best to save his people and ours." Then he asked quietly, "What is it, Saraste'?'"

It is Iella," Adia said. "Her grief, the horror at what she witnessed; it was too much. She lost their offspring."

Adia watched as Acaraho struggled to maintain control. She was also wracked with guilt. If she had not made the Guardian promise to stay with An'Kru, Pan could have stopped it. She could have saved them all.

Acaraho turned against the wall to hide his pain, his fists hard against the rock.

"I must go to the Far High Hills," Adia added. "I must tell Tehya in person. But how am I going to do it? I cannot bear to see her pain, too.

Nimida gingerly approached them, and for the first time, Adia heard the word she had waited all her life to hear her daughter say.

"Mama," Nimida cried as she fell into Adia's arms. "I never got to know him. I am grateful my last words with him were not angry ones, but I will never know him now. And I wonder how this will impact Nootau?"

"We will not know until Nootau returns from Lulnomia." Adia gently rubbed her daughter's back as she held her.

Though not everyone grieved Khon'Tor's death, enough did. Enough that Kthama's halls echoed with wails and prayers, as did those of Ktsh'Wea. They continued on into the night, and the sound carried into the verdant hills and valleys.

Adia needed to be alone. She left and walked the steep path to the meadow above Kthama. The one in which the Guardian generator stones stood. She knelt in the soft grass, closed her eyes, and, in words that came out of her mouth but had no known meaning, cried out to the Great Mother from the deepest part of her soul.

When she opened her eyes, she was no longer in the sacred meadow.

CHAPTER 16

First light had broken over the horizon, gently lighting up the hills and valleys surrounding Kthama. Adia found herself standing on the path that led down to the Great River. There was an empty water gourd in her hand. What was happening?

The most beautiful blue bird landed in a tree ahead of her and cocked its head, looking at her with first one eye and then the other.

This has happened before. How could she be there, experiencing something that had taken place in the past? What about the horror they had just learned of?

Suddenly everything shifted. Adia became dizzy, almost losing her balance. She reached out to a nearby tree for support. Her other hand went to her forehead, and she closed her eyes, waiting for the moment to pass. After a brief while, she was able to open them again.

A blinding white shimmer was solidifying in front of her. She closed her eyes again and thought, *Pan?* But if it was Pan coming to her, this time it was different.

She finally dared to look again and gasped, "How can this be?"

Standing in front of her, in Etera's morning light, stood An'Kru. Not in the Corridor. Not in the Dream World. Here, in front of her. Flesh and blood. And yet so much more.

His powerful frame towered over her. He was the size of a Sassen, though formed like the People. Adia stared at his chest and forearms and his torso, all covered in the same thick silver-white coat as Pan's, a coat that was far thicker than that of the other Akassa. His eyes were the Guardian's steel grey. A soft breeze lifted his long, flowing silver-white hair.

The powerful essence emanating from him nearly overwhelmed her. She stared at him in wonder, speechless.

"Hello, Mother," An'Kru said.

"How can this be? You left only recently with Pan —as a young offspring."

"What you remember is a ripple on what you perceive as the moving river of time, a possibility based on the actions of others. Like all the Great Spirit's creations, I have free will. And so I have returned here, at this point in time, to set things right."

"So I am not mistaken; this did happen before? I was here and the blue bird did visit me?" Adia struggled to try to remember what events had or had not happened at the point when the blue bird appeared. Her hand went to her forehead. "So you are telling me you have the ability to turn back time and change what has happened?

"Yes, Mother. The prayers of the brokenhearted, here at Kthama and at Zuenerth, and the blood of the innocent crying up from where they fell did not go unnoticed. And just as each Akassa, Sassen, Brother, and every other sentient being has free will, so do I."

PLEASE READ

Dear Readers,

I realize this was perhaps a tough read, and I hope you won't hate me for the emotional journey I just took you on. But there is one current that I trust has run through all of these books, including the ending of this one—that hope is always there to remind us that all is seldom ever truly lost.

That hope may, at times, seem to be only the width of a mere thread. Or a faint flicker in the oppressive dark. A soft voice amid the silence, almost out of range. But it is there.

And even if all is lost, there is still our hope in the love and mercy of the Great Spirit. And that thread never breaks. That flame never is extinguished. That voice never stops whispering our names.

If you enjoyed this book please consider leaving me a five star rating on Amazon, even if you do not wish to write a review.

Reviews on Goodreads are also greatly appreciated. The Goodreads address is: https://www.-goodreads.com/author/show/19613286.Leigh_Roberts

If you haven't already done so, for updates, please join my newsletter at the link below:

https://www.subscribepage.com/ theeterachroniclessubscribe

Or you can follow my author page on Amazon:

https://www.amazon.com/Leigh-Roberts/e/
B07YLWG6YT

You can email me at contact@leighrobert-
sauthor.com

If you have not yet done so, you can join the
private Etera Chronicles Facebook group!
https://www.facebook.com/groups/398774871015260

However you decide to join me, I do hope you
will. I love hearing from you, and I appreciate your
feedback and comments.

Thank you! See you in Book Three of Series
Three, Intervention!

Blessings - Leigh

ACKNOWLEDGMENT

For Richard and Bobby, who I will love forever.